Life & Death at K&A
A Collection of Short Stories

BERNARD IRVING

To Liz, Alison & Gail

Other works by Bernard Irving

The Albatros
Secrets of the Past
Spring Journey
Nightmares and Memories
Episodes in a Life (The Stories of Steven Langley)

Life and Death at K & A
Cover by: Alison Polsky
Edited by: Charles Keen, Mike Cohen

This book is a work of fiction. All characters and events portrayed in this novel are products of the author's imagination and are fictitious.

Table of Contents

Life and Death at K & A

He remembered her face. He saw it as clearly in his mind as he would see his own when he looked into a mirror. He remembered Jo's pretty features from her thin lips, curling up into a smile, to her deep brown eyes that glowed when she was happy. He remembered her straight brown hair, seemingly unruffled by the wind. He remembered how her hair felt as he would curl its long strands around his fingers. He remembered how the shimmering locks felt silken against his rough hands, softening them as if touched by magic. He remembered so much about her that he couldn't believe she was gone.

He remembered how she looked two days ago when he had met her at the base of the El steps at K&A on the day he returned home from Vietnam. He remembered how she seemed to slow as she descended the steps when he came into her view. Her eyes seemed to widen then, his unexpected presence surprising her. He remembered how her slender body seemed to hesitate on the steps, growing suddenly uneasy as she moved closer to him and finally wrapped her arms around him.

"You're back," she whispered in his ear as she pressed against him. Her body seemed to shudder as if possessed by a sudden chill even though it was a warm summer afternoon. "Jack, thank God! You're back."

Jack remembered how they had spent that night and the next day together. He remembered the passion as they entangled their bodies with one another in blissful ecstasy. He could still taste her salty skin on his lips as they became reacquainted with each and every inch of each other's bodies. He could still feel her warmth. He could still sense her joy. He could still hear her voice in his head.

It all seemed to fade instantly away to a cold eerie chill as he realized there was no warmth in her body anymore. Now, as she lay on a cold slab in the police morgue, as he saw the coroner cover her serene face with the sheet, he realized that she was gone from his life, forever.

"Yes," he gulped out the words as his mouth felt dry, full of cotton. "That's her. That's Joanne Markham."

"Could you come with me, Sir," the sergeant ordered as he took Jack's arm and escorted him from the frigid morgue.

Jack's mind drifted off, losing its sense of reality as he was pulled around the Roundhouse. All he could think about was Jo, and how she cried as they parted that night.....last night. All he could remember were the tears flowing from her eyes and down her cheeks.

"I have to go, Jack," she moaned as he begged her to stay with him. "It's work and I made a promise. I have to go."

Where was she going on a dark, rainy Friday night? Why was it so important? Why was there a fear in her eyes as she moved away from his embrace? What, Jack wondered, had a hold of her? What secret rendezvous that she had to keep could have driven her away from him after so long without him?

As Jack shook himself back to reality, He realized he was sitting in a chair in a small, cluttered office. Jack sensed cigarette smoke around him, and the strong smell of coffee filled his nostrils. Yes, he did need a smoke. Yes, he could use a cup of coffee.

He heard the snap of a match and saw the orange and yellow flame glimmer before his eyes. He felt the thin round cigarette in his fingers and then the smoke filling his lungs.

Come on! A deep voice seemed to crowd into his mind. *Snap out of it.*

His eyes began to focus on the face across the desk from him. It grew from the cloud of browns and grays and suddenly took human form. It was a thin face, large eyebrows and eyes, and a day's growth of beard. It was not his face, Jack realized, but it was familiar.

"Jack, are you okay?" the man's deep voice asked.

He nodded as he sought the familiar name that went with the familiar face. "Sure, M...Matt....I'm okay."

Matt Reamer smiled.

Jack remembered Matt Reamer. He remembered him from the neighborhood. He remembered him as a sometime friend, sometime acquaintance and sometime adversary from his youth. He remembered him from when they went to school together, played ball together, sneaked into the Midway movie house together. He remembered his surprise when he found out Matt had entered the police academy. He lost track of him after that....until now.

"I'm sorry, Jack, but I've got to ask you some questions," Matt began. "You were one of the last people to see Jo alive."

Jack nodded.

"Maybe you can help us find out who killed her."

Killed her! The words rang in Jack's brain, rattling through his consciousness as he thought about Jo. Who'd want to kill Jo? Who'd want to take away the girl he loved.

"When did you get back, Jack?" Matt asked.

"Two days ago," Jack collected his thoughts. "Flew in that morning from California after my discharge and took a cab home. I called the number my brother had for Jo, but her roommate said she was working, some place downtown. She told me that Jo usually got off the El at around five. I was there."

"How long since you'd seen each other?" Matt asked.

"We saw each other last night."

"No. Before that. Before you got back."

Jack shrugged. "Oh, it's been more than a year. We wrote some, but I was in 'Nam for a year and I wasn't much of a writer, you know. I think she thought I forgot about her."

"She was happy to see you?" Matt asked.

"Yeah.....sure."

"Why'd you let her go out that night?" Matt asked. "Didn't you know where she was going?"

Jack shook his head.

"You didn't know?" Matt repeated.

"Who killed her, Matt?" Jack asked the police detective, his voice choking. "Who would want to kill her."

"She'd been working at a sleazy bar on Arch Street. Topless place.....dancing and ....err...other things. We're asking around, but we've got no quick answers."

Jack inhaled deeply. The surprised look on his face alerted Matt Reamer that Jack didn't know what Jo was up to.

"Wake up, Jack. It's 1970. Things are tough down here," Matt said. "Some of the girls pick up some extra money stripping in the private clubs. A clerk's job downtown just doesn't cut it for girls like Jo and her friends. Who knows what those guys who run those joints talk these girls into? The girls want nice things and this gives it to them. It gets easy for them, but I guess not easy enough to tell their old boyfriend about it, especially one just back from 'Nam."

Matt Reamer couldn't look Jack in the eyes. He stared at the report in front of him and mumbled. "Sex and drugs.....the same old story."

* * * *

Jack Ceintowski grew up at K&A. It was the center of his life and the center of this working class Philadelphia neighborhood of Kensington. To outsiders it was just a stop on the elevated train to downtown. Kensington and Allegheny Avenues, K&A, was a place foreign to those from the Northeast, or from West Philly or from Jersey, but to the people down there, it focused their life. Like Jack, they remembered each place, how it fit into their lives and what they did there. Each sound had a special meaning, each place a special memory.

Two years in the army, one of them in Vietnam, hadn't shaken Jack's memories of K&A. He remembered the sound of the El going by. Every few minutes the train would pass overhead, but the sound would fade from the forefront of his mind. He noticed when it wasn't there, like the time the PTC went on strike.

He remembered better times when he had stood at the busy intersection with his friends and watched the people go by. The marble facade of the bank on the corner was perfect for this. They'd boost themselves up on the ledge and dangle their feet against the side of the building. They'd talk about the Phils. They'd look at the girls. They'd meet their buddies there and then go across the street to Wimpy's and have a burger and play some pinball.

He remembered taking the trolley car down from his home in Port Richmond and getting off at the El stop. He remembered getting coffee or a piece of pie from the Horn and Hardart Automat on Allegheny Avenue. He remembered walking Jo to the H&H after school when she worked there. He remembered every step of their teenage romance, the pecking kisses on the street and the passion in the darkness.

But that was when they were kids. Jack knew he wasn't a kid anymore and so much had changed. As he stood at K&A, his mind still shocked by the events of that Saturday morning, he noticed that the place was a little shabbier than he remembered. He noticed that there was more trash on the sidewalk, that the people looked at him differently, as if he were out of place. He knew he'd work hard to get out of that neighborhood, he knew that from the first day out of high school. Every day when he was in Vietnam he thought about moving up from the neighborhood, to Mayfair or to the suburbs. Every day!

Only then, when he dreamed, Jo was always in his plans. Now, that can never be.

Matt Reamer had told him to forget about it. There was nothing he could do, the young detective insisted. The police would do what they could to find Jo's killer, but it was police business......not something Jack should take into his own hands. But Jack Ceintowski knew they wouldn't try real hard. Jo Markham was just another statistic in a city full of crime.

Jack had to find some answers for himself. He knew where to start.   He had been told that Aura, one of Jo's roommates, would pass by K&A late Saturday afternoon.

Aura Williams was a pretty girl with a strange name and she stood out in any crowd. He remembered her glimmering blond hair that hung around her shoulders. He remembered her sparkling green eyes and her smile. He remembered her as the prettiest girl in the neighborhood, unapproachable by any of the boys. He remembered her as his friend, as Jo's friend.

He saw her walking down the street toward him, her pink flowered dress making her the brightest thing on the avenue. She passed the music store and crossed the small side street as she walked toward him. As she saw him eyeing her she stopped, her tall, thin frame quickly turning away and retracing her steps back up the street.

"Wait a minute, Aura," Jack said as he trotted up to her. "We have to talk."

Her pace increased, but he easily kept up with her.

"Let's go somewhere to talk," he insisted.

"We have nothing to talk about, Jack," she insisted in her familiar deep, sultry voice.

"Yes, we do."

"There's nothing I can say," she seemed anxious as she spoke, her voice breathless, her eyes glancing around the crowded street. "I can't bring Jo back."

"You can help me find out who and why."

"That's the police's job. Let Reamer and his friends handle it."

Jack grabbed her arm and pulled into a doorway. "Look, Aura, I loved her. I can't let it go without knowing the truth. You've got to help me find out the truth."

Aura eyes looked deeply into his. Jack could see tears in them. "What's the truth, Jack? Could you ever know? You disappeared when Jo needed you the most. Now you want the truth."

Aura was right. The truth did hurt. He knew he had let Jo down. He knew he probably shared some responsibility for what happened to her life, but he had to know more to understand his role in Jo's fate. He had to learn it from Aura.

"Look," he said as he looked down at the ground. "Is there anywhere we can go and talk? You've got to help me, Aura. You knew her better than anyone. You had to know what she was doing."

Aura stared up at the sky and bit her lip. "I knew, Jack. I got her involved in my mess. I know and it hurts."

"Come on, Aura.....tell me the truth. Are you involved in this, too?" Jack asked.

"Not here," she said as she looked suspiciously up and down the street. "Can't talk here."

* * * *

Aura Williams took Jack back to her place. It was a crowded two bedroom apartment above a storefront on the avenue. Like most of the old places on Kensington Avenue, the apartment was above the store and had a separate entrance. One time, not too long ago, most of these storefronts housed a business and the families of the people who ran them. Today, the store-owners were moving out, renting the top floors and coming in from the suburbs to run their shops only during the day.

Who knows who used to live here before, but now it was the home that reflected the three girls who lived there - Jo, Aura, and Carol Ann McGuire, longtime friends, who shared the rent and the place reflected all their moods. Surprisingly, it reminded Jack mostly of Jo.

Jack sat at the kitchen table and took his first gulp from a can of beer. Aura, who had changed into jeans and a tank top, walked nervously around the kitchen as she talked about Jo.

"She saved me," Aura began to explain. "Jo saved me. About six months ago I got into trouble, big financial trouble with a guy I had borrowed money from. Neither Jo nor Carol Ann had the money to bail me out. Every day I seemed to owe this guy more and more money."

"A loan shark?" Jack questioned.

"Yeah, well....you know how it is," Aura explained further. "When my folks died I had bills I couldn't pay. Jeez....I'm only twenty years old. What did I know? I borrowed from this guy when he offered, but couldn't pay him back."

"So he made you a deal."

She shook her head. "He told me that he'd forget the money if I'd work at a club for him. I was desperate. He offered me an answer, but didn't tell me everything. First it was just waiting tables, then dancing, then......then," Aura stared off into space, her eyes remembering. "Then it got easier. It got easier to take my clothes off for those guys. Nameless faces in the dark. Take it off, Aura! Sure, Aura, you can get a few extra bucks in a back room. Every time I turned around it was a little sleazier... a little more degrading. But the bills never got paid."

"What about Jo?" Jack asked. "How'd she get involved?"

"Yeah.....well, after a while he started pressuring me to pay him more," Aura continued. "So I went to Jo and told her what I was doing. To help me out, she went to him and made a deal with him. The same deal as me."

"And you still owed him?"

She nodded.

"What about Carol Ann? Does she know?"

"We dragged her into this, too," Aura said. "This guy, he promised that we'd be clean by the end of summer. I didn't believe him for a minute."

"Do you think he killed Jo?"

She shrugged.

"Who is he and where can I find him?"

"You know him," Aura seemed surprised at Jack's ignorance. "It's Mike Burke."

* * * *

The smell of beer filled Jack's nostrils the moment he entered the tap room. Like most of the old bars in the neighborhood, the small room was darkened and it took Jack's eyes a few minutes to adjust and for him to make out the mahogany bar that circled the center of the room. The man eyeing him from behind the bar looked typically like a bartender for this working-class neighborhood. He was heavyset and hairy, all except for the top of his head. He looked as if he took one for himself for each one he poured for a customer.

The place wasn't busy, typical for a Monday afternoon. There were two or three older men at the bar. The juke was playing some old, mellow tune and the clang of bells erupted intermittently from the pinball machine in the back corner.

Jack Ceintowski seldom frequented bars, even when he was in Saigon, but the flavor of the neighborhood bars always intrigued him.   There was one on almost every corner of these old neighborhoods and, in the summertime, they kept their doors open. Jack remembered that same sour smell crossing his nostrils every time he passed them, as strong outside as it was in here.

"You want something, Bud?" the bartender asked as Jack leaned into the padded armrest.

"Whatever's on tap," he answered as he studied his surroundings.

The bartender quickly poured the brew into a tall schooner glass and placed it in front of Jack. "Four bits," he said.

"Seen Mike Burke?" Jack asked as he tossed the coins onto the bar.

The bartender gestured toward the back, where the pinball machine chimed repeatedly.

Grabbing the beer, Jack slowly made his way toward the machine and to the back of the unsuspecting soul playing it. From the back, it didn't look like Burke. Jack remembered him as a short, skinny kid who weaseled his way through life. The man at the pinball seemed to have grown taller, broader, and had lost some of his hair. Even from the back Jack could tell he was balding, slicking down what was left to cover his scalp.

As Jack moved toward the side of the pinball the profile of Mike Burke came into view. The features were like what Jack remembered, but it was an older, weather-beaten face.

"Burke?" Jack asked as he placed his glass on the pinball machine's glass top.

"Yeah," the man said without looking up. He was concentrating on the single steel ball bouncing between the flickering bumpers.

"I want to talk to you."

"Later, man," Burke sneered, his eyes still looking down. "I'm busy."

"No. Now!" Jack said as he slammed his fist against the side of the machine. It tilted immediately.

"What's wrong with you, man!?" Burke asked as he finally looked up from the pinball machine. His mouth opened wide, but nothing came out.

"You son-of-a....." Jack started to say, but the need to punch out Mike Burke overcame his intention to stay calm. He raised up his fist and slammed it into the man's jaw.

Burke reeled backward and Jack reached out to hold him within an arm's length and slammed his fist into his jaw again. Blood squirted out of Burke's mouth.

Jack suddenly felt a jarring pain in his ribs as Burke struck back and Jack felt himself letting go of the man.

"Hey!" the voice of the bartender resounded around the room. "You guys!"

Jack felt the man's sizable hand grab him and saw him grab Burke in the same way. In the bartender's muscular grasp, Jack suddenly found his head hitting Burke's. "Take it outside!" the bartender growled.

A moment later both Burke and Jack were outside in the alley behind the bar, more stunned at the bartender's ability to take them both out than from the pain in their heads.

Jack quickly recovered his senses and grabbed Mike Burke by the shirt collar. He slammed him into the wall.

"What's the matter with you?" Burke whined. "Who are you?"

"You don't remember me?"

Burke looked stunned and confused. "No, man!"

"I'm Jack Ceintowski." Jack growled. "Remember now." He slammed him again against the wall and Burke's head bounced off the bricks as if he were one of those dolls people put in the back window of their cars.

"Yo! Let me go!" Burke hollered. "I didn't kill her, man! I didn't!"

He looked into Burke's frightened eyes. He saw the truth and loosened his grip. "The cops questioned me all day yesterday," Burke pleaded. "I proved it to them and I can prove it to you."

"Then who did?" Jack asked. "If you didn't kill Jo, who could have? Who?"

"Like I told them.... I don't know."

Jack tightened his grip again. "Listen to me, you little piece of.......Listen! The girls.... they owe you nothing....do you hear! Aura's debt is clear. If you lay your scummy hands on those girls again, I'll kill you."

"What are you talking about, man?"

"Aura told me why she's working for you and I'm telling you that her debt's now paid.... you hear!" Jack slammed him into the wall one last time. "They ain't working for you anymore."

"I don't know where you get your information, but you got it wrong," Burke said as Jack eased up on him. He straightened himself out. "Look, man, I set them up and I take my share, but they want to do this. They make good money at it, too. Especially Jo. Man, she was the best."

Jack felt the anger build up inside him once more. It was more intense than any he had ever experienced, even more than when he was in-country in 'Nam. He felt his fists clench and felt himself pound Burke's face again and again until the man collapsed on the ground before him.

Jack breathed deeply as the anger subsided leaving, the bloody mess of Burke's unconscious face staring up at him.

"Jack!" He heard a girl's voice behind him. "Jack! Stop!"

He turned and saw Carol Ann McGuire standing at the entrance to the alley. At least he thought it was her. Her dark eyes were still the same, as was her small, turned up nose and her mouth, but she was dressed in a tight miniskirt and looked cheap. The dumpy, little man next to her was old enough to be her father.

"Jack....no more," she seemed to whisper. The sound of her voice calmed him.

She looked at Jack and then at her companion. She whispered something in his ear. He nodded and walked away.

Carol Ann turned to Jack and smiled. "Long time, no see."

* * * *

"Come downtown with me," Carol Ann had begged him. "Keep me company."

Reluctantly, Jack agreed and was happy he did.

There was something about the smile that lit up Carol Ann's face as she looked at him. There was something about her eyes and the way she swayed as the El train swayed. There was something about the way she seemed to dance with the pole in the middle of the half-empty El car as it rumbled its way toward center city.

"Jeez, it's good to see you," Carol Ann said as she surveyed him. "You look good."

As she smiled at him, twirled around him, flirted with him, Jack began to forget about the hurt and anger that had consumed him. He began to forget about Jo.

After the El turned into a subway, they got off at 11th street and walked in the windy twilight toward Arch Street. The cool breeze invigorated Jack as Jo's memory and her murder drifted further and further toward the back of his mind.

"This is it, Jack," Carol Ann chirped as she took Jack's hand. "Come on up. Stay with me until it's time."

She took him through the front door of a small little hole-in-the wall bar along Philly's sleaziest strip. The place reeked of booze and the air was clouded with smoke. It wasn't the place for Carol Ann, Jack thought. It wasn't the place for any of them.

Carol Ann winked at a dirty old man who stood by the door to the back of the bar and pulled Jack with her. The dirty old man stared at her butt as she passed by and smiled at Jack but didn't stop her from taking him into the back room. The room was cold, it's walls coated with chipped paint. The small mirror was cracked and the light bulb that swung on a cord of electric wire was bright and harsh.

"Well?" Carol Ann seemed surprised at the look of disgust on Jack's face. "What did you expect?"

He shook his head. "You're better than this, Carol Ann. So's Jo and Aura. How'd you come to this?"

She smiled, her warmth taking away the cold chill of the room. "It's not so terrible, Jack. Look, the way I see it, I do this for a while after we clear Aura and I can put away enough for school. I'd never made enough working at Strawbridge's. This way I make enough to get out.... forever."

"But look what you have to do."

She continued to smile. "It's not all that bad.... really! The guys out there are harmless old men."

"One of those guys out there probably killed Jo."

The smile vanished from her face. She turned away and moved toward the small bathroom in the corner. "I wish that never happened, but I can't make it go away and I can't stop living my life."

Jack stared at himself in the mirror. He looked tired, more tired than he ever remembered, even after several weeks in-country. "Carol Ann?" he called to her. "Was this where Jo was working last weekend?"

"No," she answered from behind the bathroom door. "I don't think so. I think she was doing a private club."

"Private club?"

"Yeah, there's lots of them around town. The guy who owns this place sometimes books the girls into them."

"What's the difference?" Jack asked. "What's the difference between the private clubs and this place?"

Carol Ann emerged from the washroom. She was wearing a tight black halter top, a black leather mini shirt and long black stockings. She looked gorgeous, but cheap as a bad suit. "They're looser. Things go on there.... well, you know."

"Ever worked the private clubs?" Jack asked.

Carol Ann nodded her head. "We all did. Jo, she liked the extra cash. Jack, I hate to tell you this, but Jo liked this whole gig. She wasn't sitting around waiting for Jack Ceintowski to come home. I think I missed you more than she did."

Jack looked away. "You're not the first one to tell me that. I kind of wonder if I let Jo down?"

He felt Carol Ann's hand on his arm. "You didn't let her down, Jack. She let you down. Why, if I had someone like you I'd have waited," she said as she pulled on his arm and turned him toward her. She reached up, extending herself on her tiptoes and kissed him lightly. Her sparkling eyes stared into his and she smiled and kissed him again.

"Time, Honey!" a voice called as there was a rap on the door.

"I got to go on," Carol Ann purred. "Wait for me......please."

Jack followed her as she went out to the front of the bar. The music began to blare from a crackling old sound system. The thumping pulsating beat of The Who echoed throughout the room as Carol Ann took her place on the small stage in the front of the place.

Jack retreated to a dark corner near the door and watched her as she began to dance to the music. The six or eight men seated at the bar that made up the edge of the stage moved their drinks out of the way of her feet as she approached. They leered up at her. She looked down at them, the same wide, excited smile on her face for them as she had given him. The same sparkle in her eyes.

The music seemed to grow louder, the drums beating into Jack's brain as she captivated the men around the bar. She would dance a little, swaying to the rhythm, looking into the eyes of the drooling, sweaty old men and causing them to smile. Then she'd move on and repeat the process ten feet up the bar.

Carol Ann stopped for a long moment as the music changed to Neil Diamond's *Sweet Caroline*. Her eyes caught Jack's and penetrated his brain. She smiled widely, reached around to her back with her hands, unsnapped her top and took it off. Carol Ann turned and danced up further along the bar.

Jack turned away.

* * * *

Jack Ceintowski awoke with a headache the next morning. He couldn't get the image of Carol Ann out of his head. He still saw her striding atop that bar, the smoke curling around her slender body, her smile radiating around the room as the men stared at her. He still heard the music and the words to *Sweet Caroline* repeating over and over in his head.

As he walked out of his parents' house and walked toward Allegheny Avenue, he failed to notice anything or anyone around him. He was in another world, so much so that he didn't notice the dark figure that approached him from behind.

"Hey!" Jack finally heard the voice as a strong hand grabbed his arm.

Jack Ceintowski, with every muscle in his body tensing, with the training of a grunt, turned to face his attacker.

"Damn! Didn't you hear me?" Burke cringed as he backed away from Jack. "You better cool it. You're going to blow a gasket."

Jack took a deep breath and sighed. "What do you want?"

"That's better," Burke smiled. He looked a mess. He wore the battle scars of his beating from Jack. There were bandages above each eye and his black and blue face just looked like it hurt. A lot.

"Well?" Jack clenched his fist again. "What do you want?"

"I've come to warn you," Burke went on. "Like I said before, I don't know what happened to Jo. She was working a private party that night. It was a favor for a club owner. If you snoop around, he'll cut off your nose before you can blink, man. So, lay off."

"I've got to find out what happened," Jack insisted. "I'm not going to let the cops sweep her death under the rug."

"Listen, man," Burke smirked. "I'm trying to do you a favor. Why? I don't know. You've beaten me to a pulp.

You've taken away my best girls, but I feel I owe you this. Jack, this club owner is a cop. If he's involved in Jo's death, he's got it covered up good. If he's not, and I don't think he is, he's still going to keep this quiet. Man, he's got connections, so he won't want to make this public. If you go after him, it'll be trouble."

Jack nodded. "Thanks for the warning, Mike."

"Don't mention it, man," Burke said as he turned and walked away mumbling. "Don't mention it."

* * * *

He met Carol Ann in front of a small restaurant at the end of the block. She wore a loose-fitting sweatshirt and jeans that quickly erased the image of her topless dancing atop the bar from Jack's mind. She seemed like a different girl as she smiled her wide smile and wrapped her arms around him, spinning him around dizzily in the street.

"Good morning, Jack," she chirped. Her dark eyes darted across the street and ignored the looks of several passersby as she planted a wet kiss on his lips. "I'm starving."

Within minutes they were surrounded by coffee and juice, toast and eggs at a small corner booth in the restaurant. The smile never left her face and her eyes continued to stare right past him as she ate with the same kind of abandon with which she approached everything else.

Jack couldn't eat a bite.

"It doesn't bother you, does it?" he asked.

His words caught her attention and she turned from staring out the window to look curiously at him, the fork dangling from her mouth. "Huh?"

"None of it phases you," he continued. "Not the way you have to live. Not the guys gawking at you. Not the creeps you have to work for. Not Jo's death. Nothing!"

Her bright eyes darkened and she looked down at the plate of food. The smile was finally gone from her face. "Sure, it bothers me, Jack, but life does go on. I'm using those creeps to get what I want. I'm trying to survive.... yes, and to enjoy.... what I must do. I can't sit here and sulk over my fate, or Jo's fate. She was my friend, but......."

"She was more than a friend to me."

"That's your problem," she stated coldly. "I only wish, ... well.... you know."

"No, I don't know," he stared back at her and searched her face for an answer.

She took a long sip of coffee and placed the cup loudly back in its saucer. "Oh, Jack. Wake up! Jo didn't feel the same way about you as you're crying about her. It made me and Aura sick just to listen to her laugh about you. She'd get your letters from 'Nam and read them out loud to us and then laugh, crumple them up and toss them away. She was having a good time and didn't want some all too serious soldier-boy cramping her act. She couldn't care less."

Jack couldn't believe what Carol Ann was telling him. He remembered the letters he got from her while over there, few though they were. He remembered the words that spilled out on those pages, words that said she still loved him.

"You were the one we felt sorry for," Carol Ann continued. "Aura and I hated the way she pushed you aside. I always thought you were something special, someone too good for Jo."

"What?" he was dazed by her words. "But when she saw me......"

"Yeah, I know, it all came back," Carol Ann looked up at the ceiling. "She saw you at K&A and suddenly fell in love with you again. Well, don't believe it for a moment. Sure, she was glad you were back. Sure, she was happy you came home alive and maybe there was some spark left, but it wouldn't have lasted long. If she hadn't died she'd have dumped you for some quick thrill, for anything that came along."

"No, you're wrong."

"You're blind," Carol Ann then realized. "You can't see the truth." She stood up from the booth, stared down at him as a tear rolled down her cheek. "I can't make you see the truth. Good-bye, Jack."

She bolted from the restaurant. Jack left some money on the table and followed her as she ran down the street toward her apartment. He caught up to her at the door, reached out and grabbed her.

As they pressed together she brought her lips up to his and kissed him. Jack tried to feel nothing, but he soon found himself lost in her kiss.

"Oh, Jack." she whimpered as she melted into his arms. "I love you."

* * * *

The phone rang on the table beside the bed. It brought Jack Ceintowski back from his empty thoughts as he lay cuddled up with Carol Ann. As both jumped at the sound, Jack instinctively reached for the receiver.

"No. I'll get it," Carol Ann said as she reached over him, laying her body across his. "Maybe it's Aura. She's probably wondering where I am."

Jack smiled at her and received her warm smile in reply. Her eyes then turned toward the phone, but her body didn't move from on top of him. "Hello," she said and then listened to the caller.

"Uh-huh," she murmured, her eyes curiously darting between the wall and Jack's own stare.

"Who is it?" he asked.

"Uh-huh," she just repeated.

"Is it Aura, or someone else?"

"Okay. Eight o'clock," Carol Ann said and then placed the receiver back in its cradle.

"Who was that?" Jack immediately asked.

The girl rolled over and lay next to him on the bed, her eyes staring blankly up at the ceiling.

"Well?"

"It was someone I know," she softly said. "It was the man who owns the private club in Fishtown. The one where they found Jo's body."

Jack lifted himself up and rested on his elbow. "What did he want?"

"He wants me to work tonight."

"And you agreed."

She nodded and turned her eyes toward Jack. "Yes."

"Why? I don't want you doing that anymore, especially not there."

"I'm doing this for you," she said. "Maybe it will help us find some answers."

* * * *

Jack watched Aura Williams as she danced on the small stage at the center of the darkened room. The club pounded with the vibrating sounds of rock-n-roll, some tune Jack vaguely recognized, but couldn't place. The lights around the stage flashed on and off without regard to the beat as Aura danced before the dazed and drunken spectators.

As always, she inspired a gaping numbness to the men around her. Her brilliant eyes, her dazzling blond hair, her round, perfect face was all that Jack could see. That most of the men who gawked at her weren't looking at her beautiful face was understandable. Aura was the sixth dancer of the night and the men still concentrated on her body as it swayed before them. All but Jack, he ignored it, almost avoiding looking at her in that way to not spoil the image.

She turned as the music reached its climax so that all the men could see was her back as her body kept time with the beat. Then the song faded away to cheers that echoed throughout the room. The lights dimmed ever so slightly and Aura disappeared backstage.

The music began up again. *Sweet Caroline* played and Carol Ann appeared and Jack turned away again, unwilling to look at her as she danced. There was something unsettling about the way Carol Ann danced. There was something unsettling as she stared at each face, as her smile locked in on each man's eyes, as she seemed to enjoy it so much.

He backed out of the room and saw Aura standing there, slightly out of breath and staring at him. She ran her tongue along the edge of the tall glass of coke and gave him a leering wink. He felt drawn to her.

"Was I good tonight?" she asked as she reached out for his hand.

"I don't know how to judge," he answered. "It's strange to see girls I've known for so long up there.... like that."

As she led Jack into the back room of the place the light became harsher, glaring from the unprotected light bulbs that lined the walls. She had covered herself with a simple white tee-shirt and her figure showed through as she passed nearer the light.

In the far corner of the room, where no one looked and where the music and the hoots from the spectators could barely be heard, Aura wrapped herself around Jack and snuggled close to him. "When I go up there, afterwards, I feel so warm, so good."

Jack instinctively felt himself drawn to and excited by her, yet his mind told him to withdraw.

"Tonight, I saw you there and I felt more excited than ever," she purred as she licked his ear. "Tonight, I danced for you, Jack."

Somehow, despite what he had felt for Jo, what he now felt for Carol Ann, Aura just seemed to capture him. He kissed her and felt himself entrapped by her.

"I always wanted you, Jack," she murmured in his ear. "It was always so tough for me, you know. I know what they said, what you said......I was the prettiest girl in the neighborhood. I was off limits....to everyone and I was lonely. Didn't you know I was lonely, Jack?"

He shook his head.

"I was so jealous of Jo," she continued as she pressed herself against him, her voice nearly panting out the words. "Everyone looked at Aura, but didn't touch. Even you, but you went to Jo and stayed with her, even when she didn't want you anymore."

He broke away from her grasp. "I heard enough of that and I won't believe it. Jo did love me."

"It was over before you went away, Jack," Aura said, her eyes continuing to beckon him closer. "She just figured you'd forget about her, or get yourself killed. She ignored every letter you sent."

"That's a lie! She wrote me back."

"No, Jack," Aura smiled at him. "That was me. I wrote you back, every letter you received was from me."

He shook his head in disbelief.

"I can show you your letters, Jack. I took them from the trash can where Jo put them even before she read them. I can prove it to you."

He forced himself to break away from her. He forced his eyes to break contact with hers and walked away in disgust, no longer knowing who to trust or believe.

"I loved you, Jack," Aura's crying voice faded away as he left. "I still do."

Jack needed some fresh air. The cool night felt good as it entered his lungs, clearing his mind of the confusing thoughts. Did Aura really write those letters? Did Jo really not care? "I'm no stud," he mumbled to himself. "What do these women see in me?"

He heard an El train rumble off in the darkness and tried to understand. He remembered those lonely and desperate letters he wrote to Jo. He remembered her passionate and loving response and remembered how much he felt she had changed. How much the letters were not like her. Now, he knew. He felt like a fool but, damned, he still cared for Jo. He still needed to know who murdered her!

He felt a tap on his shoulder that startled him and brought him back from his thoughts. He turned quickly and felt an angry mask cover his face as he looked at Matt Reamer.

"Are you okay?" Reamer asked with a genuine look of concern in his voice.

"What are you doing here?" was all Jack could ask.

"I was going to ask you the same thing?"

"I came with Carol Ann McGuire," he said. He felt uncomfortable even saying her name to the young detective.

"Why?" he seemed overly curious. "You never seemed like the type of guy for this type of place."

"I'm probably here for the same reasons you are, Reamer," Jack snapped back at him. "This is where Jo was murdered."

He shook his head. "No, Jack. This is the place where her body was found. That's all, and we've closed the investigation, temporarily."

"What!"

"You heard me, Jack. We've closed it down and you shouldn't be interested anyway. Who do you think you are anyway, Mannix?" Reamer smirked at him.

Suddenly angry, Jack grabbed Matt Reamer by the lapels of his jacket and slammed him against the wall. "I knew you cops would do that. I knew you couldn't care less who killed her."

Reamer pushed Jack away. "Calm down, Jack! I've got no say in this. Higher ups closed this thing down. You don't know what you're messin' with."

Jack composed himself and looked around at the deserted street. "I think the owner here had something to do with it, and I'm going to prove it!" he whispered.

Reamer laughed. "No way!"

"How do you know?"

"Because, I know," he continued to laugh. "Trust me, Jack. You couldn't be more wrong."

Jack felt the anger continue to grow inside him. Reamer may be a cop, he may have Jack thrown in jail, but he was mocking him and Jack couldn't allow that. He formed his hands into fists and glared at the man, who was still simply amused at Jack's accusations.

"Jack!" Carol Ann's voice called behind them. "Matt! Stop it!"

Both men turned to face the girl, who stood in the doorway, her face glaring back at both of them with coldness. She quickly placed herself between them.

She stared up at Matt Reamer. "Let him alone. He doesn't know what he's talking about."

"Carol Ann, you stay out of this," Jack snapped at her as he grabbed her shoulder and tried to force her out of the way.

Showing surprising strength, she held her ground.

"Your Dad wants to see you, Matt," she said to him. "One of the customers is getting out of hand."

Reamer looked at her and then at Jack. "Okay....okay. I'm going in, but you better straighten him out, Doll. You better straighten him out."

Reamer turned and disappeared into the club.

Carol Ann turned to Jack, her engaging smile returning as she looked up at him. "Jeez, you are a hot head. What did you think you were doing?"

She touched her hand against his hot skin and Jack felt suddenly calmer. She looked at him with a soft and knowing smile.

"I thought we were here to find something out?" Jack asked.

"We are," Carol Ann continued. "If it'll make you happy."

"I thought the owner of this place would be a good place to start," Jack said. "Reamer just laughed at me."

Carol Ann smiled. "That's because his old man and him own the place."

"Reamer's old man is a cop," Jack remembered.

She nodded. "Uh-huh, and Matt's partners with him now. Neither of them did anything to Jo except find her in the back room, her skull smashed in."

"How do you know all this?"

Her eyes sparkled as they observed his bewilderment. "I just do. But that's not the point here, Jack. Someone did it. Someone who could be alone with Jo in the back room and not raise suspicion."

"So, we're closer."

"Uh-huh."

"Closer than the cops," he snapped. "They've closed the books."

Her smile broadened. "What would you expect? Two quite proper policemen own a strip joint in Fishtown. A girl was murdered there. It'd ruin them."

He nodded. "I see."

Carol Ann reached up on her tip-toes and gave him a pecking kiss. "You just stay out here and stay calm. I'm going to ask around some more before my next show. See ya'!" she said as she turned and wiggled her way back into the bar.

* * * *

The sour smell of booze filled Carol Ann McGuire's nostrils the second she entered the darkened club. There must have been thirty middle-aged, overweight men sitting around the room with their beers, their laughter and their leers at the homely teenager who was on-stage trying her best to entertain them. The members of the club paid a lot of money for their recreation and the right to sit and leer at mostly undressed dancing girls, but it was a shame for some of the girls, like this one, too young and not quite pretty enough to hold their attention. She wouldn't be asked back, Carol Ann knew.

All in all, Carol Ann enjoyed this part time work. It paid a lot better than her day job, selling women's clothes, and offered some hope for her future as she had socked most of what she got away. If she continued after paying off Aura's debt, it could have amounted to something.

Yet, Carol Ann knew this would be her last night. She had her prize. She had Jack. Jo had been her friend, but she was gone. Aura was her friend, too, but she knew she'd listen to Jack, who was the kind of man who'd take a girl out of a bad situation. He was the kind of man who could get her out of the neighborhood, something she'd worked for so hard, but never seemed to get. K&A just kept pulling her back. It pulled her back from college, back from a respectable job downtown, back from what she saw as her future. She needed someone strong like Jack Ceintowski to pull harder than K&A.

Carol Ann had known Jack since Junior High School when they had been assigned to sit together in home room. Over the years he had matured into a tall, solid man with cool brown eyes, a sincere, clever smile and a quiet personality that seemed to say to everyone that he really knew what he was doing, even if he didn't. His quiet demeanor could put off strangers, but the people who really knew him liked him or, to somconc likc Carol Ann, lovcd him.

She smiled to herself and looked in the mirror as she entered the room backstage. It was that same smile that she knew enchanted the men around her. Carol Ann knew she had a look about her. She knew she could charm a man and loved it. She loved toying with them. She loved casting a spell over them.

In the reflection, she saw another figure lurking in the dark corner of the room. It was Aura leaning awkwardly against the wall, her eyes dejectedly looking downward. Something was wrong, Carol Ann knew, and her heart began to pound inside her chest.

"Aura?" she asked as she approached. "What's the matter?"

"I've lost," Aura mumbled as she weakly moved her head up to face Carol Ann. There were tears in her eyes.

"What's wrong?" Carol Ann repeated. "What have you lost?"

"I've lost Jack," she said, her voice cracking. "I lost him to you."

Carol Ann held out her hand to Aura and helped her to right herself. She looked around the room to find someone to help, but the backstage room was empty. The sound of music and laughter had grown louder from up front, things were loosening up in the club as the night progressed, as it always did.

"I never meant to hurt you, Aura. You know that," Carol Ann told her friend.

"You're just like her," Aura's voice suddenly took on a nasty tone and her eyes became wide and riveted on Carol Ann. "Just like Jo. You're both so easy, just pretty enough to keep him interested. Just pretty enough to get him. You couldn't scare him off... like I do."

"Aura, what are you talking about?"

Aura's hand wrapped itself tightly around Carol Ann's wrist and a shot of pain sparked through Carol Ann's body. "I should have taken care of you before. I should have known you'd sink your teeth into him the first chance you'd get."

"What?"

"I should have killed you when I killed Jo."

Carol Ann felt frightened and had the sudden urge to run, but Aura clenched her wrist tighter, twisting it painfully. "Aura! Let me go!" she shouted at the top of her lungs.

The music seemed to grow instantly louder and drowned her out.

Aura smashed the tall glass she was holding against the wall and it shattered in her hand. She held the jagged glass bottom and brought it toward Carol Ann's face.

"It's no use now," Aura mumbled. "They'll figure it all out, you know. No use leaving you behind to pick up the pieces. No use leaving you behind for Jack. If I can't have him at least you won't."

The broken glass came nearer to Carol Ann's face. Aura's hands, covered with her own blood seemed to shake and quiver as it inched ever closer. Time seemed to stand still and Carol Ann screamed in fear.

The music pounded in her head.

The glass nicked her skin and Aura drew her hand quickly away.

"No! No! Aura! No!" Carol Ann screamed as she struggled to free herself.

The door to the room suddenly bolted open and Carol Ann saw Jack. She felt Aura's grip on her suddenly loosen as she turned to face him.

Jack just stood there, paralyzed, and stared in disbelief.

"I'm sorry, Jack," Aura cried as she pointed the jagged glass at him. "I have to do this!"

She turned again toward Carol Ann, her eyes filled with hate and madness and brought the broken glass closer to Carol Ann's neck. All Carol Ann could see was the glass as it got closer and closer.

And then it vanished.

The music got suddenly softer and Aura crumpled to the floor in tears.

Jack held the remains of the glass in his hand and tossed it into a nearby trash can. As people began to gather around and stare at Aura, a weeping lump of flesh on the floor, her bloody hand cupping her face, Jack reached down and took Carol Ann into his arms.

"I did it for you, Jack," Aura choked out the words. "I did it for you."

* * * *

K&A looked dirtier that she ever remembered. There was something in the air, a smell, or just the feeling that something had changed in the way Carol Ann felt about the neighborhood. It was different, almost alien to her as a noisy silence surrounded her.

The El rumbled into the station and squealed to a halt. She barely noticed it. A trolley car chattered down Allegheny Avenue and stopped by the concrete island as old newspapers thrown around by the breeze scurried by. Carol Ann sat silently on the cold marble ledge of the big old bank building and waited silently.

Then she saw Jack begin to cross Kensington Avenue in her direction and she felt the smile returning to her face. She had fallen in love.

Jo was forgotten. Poor Aura, the pressures of life and loneliness having destroyed her poor mind, was forgotten. All that mattered to Carol Ann was her happiness and joy at falling in love. The rest, the regret over her lost friends, the regret over the steps she willfully took that made things worse, her regret at the way she had treated herself, those would all come back and must be dealt with, but not today.

As she wrapped her arms around him and kissed him joyfully, Carol Ann knew that today was for love and plans for the future. Today was the day to plan for her future with Jack as far away from K&A as she could get.

Memories of Katie

The first time he saw Katie it was from a distance.

He had been at a training class in New York City and was on his way home. He was at Penn Station in Manhattan and standing by the gate leading to the Trenton bound train that would eventually get him back to Philly late that afternoon in October, when he spied her sitting on an old, unused baggage claim counter.

She seemed so very out of place then and there, with her legs crossed and a cigarette dangling between her fingers. She was wearing ankle length boots, jeans and a plain brown sweater… nothing out of the ordinary for a young woman in 1970. But she was so damn pretty with her long, straight sandy brown hair, riveting eyes, and a shy smile that seemed to extend from ear to ear. He just couldn't take his eyes off her.

They had both been listening to a father talking to his young son about train travel. From what he picked up from the conversation between them, this pre-teen boy was taking his first train ride with his dad and was curious about everything. The father was struggling to answer all the child's questions. By the smile on Katie's face and on his own, they both were equally amused.

"What does the train run on?" the boy was asking.

"Electricity," the father answered.

"It doesn't run on the train tracks?" the boy then asked.

"Of course it does," the increasingly frustrated father answered quickly. "I thought you meant what powered the train."

"Doesn't it burn coal?"

"It's not the old west, son."

Not wanting to be obvious or blatantly creepy, he diverted his eyes away from both the girl and the father and son. He could smell the acrid scent of the cigarette smoke that seemed to be enveloping her and found even that appealing. Still looking away, he eyed down the steps to the train platform where the train, already overdue, was supposed to be.

"Excuse me," he heard a mellow toned voice say behind him. He turned toward the sound of the voice and saw her right next to him. "Can you help me?" she then asked.

At first he wondered if she was actually talking to him as there were other people around, but in a second he realized that she was. He couldn't find the words to answer, so he just nodded his head.

"I need some help with my bags," she went on. "I was wondering if you could give me a hand?"

"Absolutely! No problem!" he almost shouted. He didn't even ask how much baggage she had. It was the furthest thing from his mind as she smiled back at him. He was simply shocked that the pretty girl had picked him out of the crowd.

"Great," she seemed to breathe a sigh of relief. "I was so worried that I wouldn't be able to handle it all. Thanks for your help in advance."

"Sure. No problem," was all that came out of his mouth.

"I'm Katie," she said as she smiled up at him. "Katie Sherman."

"Matt Michaels," he replied, adding. "A pleasure to meet you."

* * * *

The train had finally arrived at Penn Station. It was made up of several of those antiquated old rail cars that were slowly being phased out of service by Conrail. It smelled of hydraulic fluid and plastic. It seemed to groan as the people boarded and settled into its plastic covered benches, each more uncomfortable than the next one. It had seen its better days over a half century of service. Matt even suspected he might find Indian arrowheads embedded in the wood that comprised the exterior of the car.

The girl called Katie had been right to need help with her suitcases. She had three tan colored bags and each was slightly bigger and heavier than the next. Matt, as he had just one light briefcase, easily helped her with two of her three. He hoisted them all up to the shelf above their seats before sitting in the seat next to her.

"Are you going all the way down to Philadelphia?" the girl asked.

"Yes," he replied. "To 30th Street Station. How about you?"

She nodded. "Yes. Boy, am I glad I ran into you. I dreaded this trip."

"First time in Philly?" he asked. "Visiting?"

"No, actually I've been studying at Penn," she explained. "But I had to go back home for a few days. Family emergency. My dad sent me back with enough clothing to last through the next two semesters."

"Hope that everything is okay?" he asked next.

Her face took on a curious expression.

"With your family emergency, I mean," Matt completed his first thought.

Katie frowned. "Well….no, not really. My mom died just before school started and Dad wasn't taking it too well, suddenly being alone. Needed to be there with him, you understand."

Both of them lapsed into a period of silence as he could see that talking about her father had upset her. He let her be alone with her thoughts until they had passed through Newark on their way south.

Finally, she broke the icy silence.

"When we get to Trenton do we have to change trains?" she asked.

"Yes," Matt answered. "Don't worry. I've made this trip a few times. I'll take care of you."

That brought a smile back to Katie's face.

"How do you like Penn?" he then asked.

"It's okay, I guess," she answered as her smile disappeared. "With everything going haywire at home I haven't had time to enjoy campus life or Philadelphia. I'm from Chicago, so it's very different."

"Hopefully, you'll get into it now," he tried to smile back at her and not just leer at her like a teenager in heat.

"You from Philadelphia?" Katie asked, then added. "I'm sorry....but I've forgotten your name."

"Matt. Actually, Matthew Michaels," he answered. "And yeah, I'm from there."

"Why were you in New York?"

"My work sent me up for a class," he explained. "Just for the day."

"What do you do?" Katie asked as she slouched back in her seat. Both of them were becoming more relaxed as they became more familiar with each other, Matt thought.

"I'm a computer programmer with a medical company based in downtown Philly," he answered. "Just got started with them this past summer since finishing college."

"Penn?"

"No, nothing quite as Ivy League," he told her. "Temple University."

"I've heard of that, but don't know much about it."

"It's a big commuter school," he explained. "A lot of local kids. Sometimes, it seems like a big high school."

"You live in town?" she asked.

"No, not in center city. In Kensington. Just a little ride on the El from where you are," he went on to explain.

She was puzzled. "I'm not familiar with it. And what El train is that? I know there's a subway here in Philly, but not an El train. We have those in Chicago.

"We have an El, but in center city it's underground," he went on. "Have you explored the city at all?"

She shook her head.

"We'll have to change that, too," he told her. "I'll show you around."

"I'll like that," she said. "Let me give you my number."

* * * *

Katie and Matt continued to chat on the rest of their trip down to Philadelphia. Mostly they talked about nothing important, but enough for Matt to get a pretty good picture of the attractive coed sitting next to him.

Katherine Marie Sherman was fairly typical for a midwestern girl of nineteen. She had grown up comfortably in suburban Chicago as the only child of two professional parents. Her father was in insurance and her mother taught school until her untimely death in an automobile accident just before Katie started her first semester at the University of Pennsylvania. Like most nineteen year old girls, Katie had no idea what she wanted to do with her life, but a quality education would help her determine what to do next.

Matthew Michaels's life and background bore little resemblance to Katie's existence. His parents were shopkeepers in a very working class neighborhood who had scraped together enough money to send their son to college. Sometime in the past his father's family had changed their names from a very Irish McMichael to something more American and Matt grew up as a good Irish lad fitting in with his Polish and German neighbors. Matt got through growing up and through school without any major traumas in his young life and without doing anything either stupid or daring. Not particularly outgoing, the shy young man of twenty two had never seriously been involved with any girls at school. His studies came first. Now, with college over, he still found it awkward when it came to meeting girls.

To Matt, Katie seemed different, if challenging. She was easy to talk to even though he was mesmerized by the girl. As they talked he found the conversation becoming easier and easier while his eyes still were riveted on her features. She was quite pretty, he realized, without being overwhelmingly beautiful. She seemed very comfortable in her own skin.

By the time the train rolled into 30th Street Station in downtown Philly, Matt had determined to keep in contact with her. He had to learn more about the sandy haired coed with the sparkling eyes and shy smile.

He helped her with her suitcases all the way to the taxi stand outside the terminal.

"I do so appreciate all your help today, Matt," she told him as they stood in line for a cab. "I never would have been able to get here without you."

"It was my pleasure," he answered. He wanted to make sure he got her number as she had promised earlier in the trip, but felt it would be too forward to ask her for it.

"How do you get home from here?" Kate asked as she opened her small pocketbook.

"I'll get on the subway," he began.

"Which turns into the El," she interrupted. "See…I remember."

"That's right," he laughed. "I guess I taught you something about my hometown."

"And you'll have to teach me more," Katie said as she took out a notepad and a pen from her pocketbook. She quickly wrote on the notepad, tore off the page and handed it to him.

"Thanks," Matt said as he realized she was giving him her number.

"This is the number to my dorm room. It's a party line so don't be shocked if you get another coed. Please call me," she said. "I get the feeling that you can teach me a lot more about this city."

Katie put her arms around Matt, reached up and kissed his cheek. As she pulled away Matt saw the widest, most alluring smile cross her face. A split second later she was in the cab and waving back at him as the taxi sped away from the station.

Matthew Michaels waved back.

"What was that all about?" he heard from a familiar voice behind him.

Matt turned to face his friend Bob Finlay. He hadn't expected to see him then and there. It was nearly as much a surprise as Katie's kiss.

"Make a new friend on the train ride down?" he asked Matt.

Bob, who was only slightly younger than Matt and as close as a brother to him, came next to him and strained to see the girl in the rear seat of the taxi as it moved down the street.

"Didn't know you'd become a lady's man," Bob commented.

Matt smiled. "Yeah, sure! A regular Romeo!" He looked down at the piece of paper in his hand. "If she hadn't volunteered her phone number to me I'd never have gotten the nerve to ask. Big lady's man! Now I only have to get up the nerve to call it."

"Are you going to call her?" Bob asked as the two men started to walk toward Market Street.

"I plan to," Matt replied as he stuffed the phone number in his pocket.

"Well, I thought I'd come down and surprise you, but you're the one who surprised me," Bob smiled. "Right now let's go over to Cavanaugh's before happy hour ends and have a brew or two."

Matt nodded as the pair turned right onto Market Street.

* * * *

It took Matt nearly two weeks to summon up the courage to call her number. The crumpled piece of paper had remained stuffed in his jacket pocket that whole time and he could barely make out the numbers by the time he unwrapped it and made the call.

An unfamiliar voice picked up, but Matt realized that he barely remembered what Katie's voice actually did sound like. He hesitated to respond to the girl's hello.

"Hello! Hello!" she repeated. "Is anybody there?"

"A….umm," Matt stammered. "I…..I'm looking for Katie Sherman."

"She not here," the voice said back. "This is Emily. Her roommate. Is there anything I can do for you?"

"I'm…..uh….this is Matt," he continue to stammer and his throat dried up as he spoke. "I met her a couple of weeks ago on the way back from New York."

"Okay," the voice chirped in. "You're her white knight from the train. She hasn't stopped talking about you since."

That perked Matt up. Suddenly he felt more confident. "Oh, really? It wasn't much."

"Don't think that," the girl snapped back. "You don't know how hard it is to find someone to help a girl out these days. I know. I've had my own problems with stuff like that, too."

"Well," he jumped in. "I wouldn't think….."

She cut him off. "Honestly, Matt! Some guys think that if they help you cross the street you're ready to fuck them all night."

Matt hesitated to answer. "Well, I wouldn't. I never though…"

The girl giggled. "Of course you wouldn't, but that doesn't mean someone else isn't thinking that, you know."

"I guess not."

"Come on, Matt," she continued to giggle. "During that whole trip down with Katie didn't the thought of banging her cross your mind at least once?"

He was silent for a minute.

"Matt, you still there?" Emily's voice asked.

"Still here," he answered. "Just don't know how to answer that one and not sound like one of two kinds of idiots."

"Sorry I put you on the spot," she giggled back. "Sorry if I'm being too crass. I tend to just blurt out whatever's in my head."

Now Matt laughed. "Nothing wrong with that."

"Depends," she answered. "Look…..I'll tell Katie you called. Is there a number she can call you back on."

Matt thought about his mother answering Katie's callback and quickly thought otherwise. "No……I'll call her back."

"Okay," Emily answered. "I'll let her know. You sound sweet so I hope you do call her back."

After he had hung up the phone he realized how much he needed to get his own phone. He also, for the first time, thought about having sex with Katie. He tried to shake the image of her naked body on top on him, but it lingered on there, in the forefront of his thoughts......for hours.

* * * *

He did not wait long to call her back. For privacy he went to a phone booth across from work to make the call.

"Hello," the voice on the other side of the line answered. It sounded like Katie's voice as he remembered it.

"I'm Matt," he quickly answered, more confident than his prior call to the same number. "Do you remember me?"

"Certainly," she chirped back. "How could I forget you?"

"We need to get to know each other better," he said. He had trouble hiding the excitement in his voice that he had finally reached her.

"Yes, we do!" she excitedly said back.

"How about we set a date to get together?"

"Okay."

"I could come and meet you near Penn's Campus," Matt quickly answered. " Just name the day and time."

"How about Friday, four thirty."

"I'll be there!"

"Okay, but where?" she giggled, realizing his excitement.

"Yes! It would be best we find a place to meet," Matt stammered back. "Let's see.......there's a pizza restaurant at 36th and Walnut........can't remember the name."

"I know it," Katie shot back. "I'll meet you there."

As Matt hung up the phone he felt satisfied with himself. Hopefully, he will recognize her when the time comes.

* * * *

Matt was already sitting in the booth at the pizza joint when she arrived. Like most of the thousands of pizza places that were scattered all over Philadelphia it consisted of a handful tacky red vinyl covered booths perfect for two people as well as the typical mural of Venice, gondolas and all, on the walls. A couple of gleaming silver pizza ovens were in back of the counter manned by two dark haired rough looking guys in white aprons. In the background Sinatra crooned on and the smell of baked pizza dough hung in the air.

Katie looked pretty much the same girl Matt remembered from the train. Her hair was pulled back into a pony tail and she wore no makeup. Her eyes immediately trained in on Matt's booth and she walked slowly his way. She wore a pair of tight, well worn jeans and a grey sweatshirt two sizes too big. Although the weather was chilly she did not have on a coat.

She surprised Matt when she sat in the booth next to him rather than across from him. She leaned into him and lightly planted a kiss on his lips.

"Great to see you, Matt," she purred. "I thought I'd never hear from you again.

"Good to see you too," Matt almost stuttered back. She had wrapped her arm around his and clasped her hand in his interlocking their fingers. She was not going to let him get away.

"I'm starved," Katie whispered in Matt's ear. "I hope you've already ordered."

Surprisingly Matt had ordered and the steaming hot pie was being set on table as she spoke.

"Is coke okay?" he asked and she nodded. He turned to the server, "Two cokes please And thanks!" The man nodded back while he surveyed Katie pressing herself against Matt and then walked away shaking his head.

Katie took her fingers from her free hand a pressed the crust of the thin pizza. "These are so different than what I'm used to. Chicago pizza is deep dish and loaded with sauce, cheese and other goodies. This is like eating a cracker with tomato sauce."

"Thin crust is popular in Philly," he countered. "We do have some deep dish here as well. If I had known you'd preferred that I would have picked a place that had it."

"It's not that important," Katie said as she unwrapped herself from him and pulled off a piece of the steaming pizza.

Matt took her hand gently and pulled the piece of pizza away from her mouth before she could bite down on it. "Be careful," he told her. "It's still too hot to eat, at least wait for the sodas."

The cokes came moments later and Matt & Katie settled down to eating. As she ate, Katie wrapped her leg around Matt's leg and kept herself snuggled against him. Matt tried to relax and keep his mind on his meal but she continued burrowing into him and was starting to arouse him.

After the meal was consumed, she turned to Matt with a sly smile on her face. "Now what?" she asked.

Matt laughed. "I thought the food would last longer and I really hadn't thought this out past dinner."

"I have," she answered back. "My friends have an apartment nearby and I have the key."

"Sounds like a plan to me!" Matt said quickly as he placed money under the check. "Let's get out of here."

* * * *

Katie wasn't kidding. After a brisk ten minute walk in the cool night air Matt and Katie came up to the entrance of a small apartment building just off the Penn Campus.

"The upper classmen got this apartment because they can live off campus," Katie explained as she fiddled with the key to the building. "They're all Chicago people and have made the apartment available to many of the lower classman from the Chicago area like me."

She was still fumbling around with the keys and dropped them on the ground. She seemed unsteady on her feet.

Matt bent down, picked up the keys, found the right one and quickly opened the door, grasping Katie's hand and pulling her into the foyer.

"Okay, which apartment?" he asked, still holding on to the keys.

Katie started up the steps, "208, just up these stairs.

Matt opened the door to apartment 208 with the other key on her keychain. After entering, Katie pushed the door shut, turned the lock and rested herself comfortably against the back of the door.

She pulled Matt's jacket off his shoulders. "I'll take that!" she purred as her hands brought the arms of the jacket to his wrists. Instinctively Matt turned and she pulled the jacket off him and placed it onto a hook on the wall.

She then turned him back around and pulled him close, drawing her lips to his and gave him a long passionate kiss.

"Wow," Matt whispered when she finally drew her lips away. "That was a lot more than I expected."

"Oh, really," she smiled up at him. "What were you expecting?"

"I guess I was expecting a nice dinner with nice conversation as we got to know each other better."

"Where are you from? 1955?"

"No," he laughed back. "I am from 1970, but I've never been too quick with girls. Usually they intimidate me."

She sighed and unbuttoned the first couple of buttons on Matt's shirt and kissed his not so hairy chest. "Now, do I intimidate you, Matthew?"

"No," Matt whispered back. "There's something about you. From the first moment I saw you in that train station I knew there was something different about you."

She leaned up and kissed him hard as she pressed herself against him. "What did you see in me as being different?"

"I don't know," Matt answered as he kissed Katie's neck and as she turned her back to him and ran her hands through his hair. "You just looked different."

"How different?" She moaned as he nuzzled his mouth into her neck.

"Mysterious," he answered as he kissed her neck again. "Sultry."

"Oh sure!"

Matt continued to kiss her neck as he ran his hands up inside her sweatshirt to her breasts. As he caressed her she gasped and her body moved with each motion of his hands.

"Wait," Katie moaned as she broke away from his arms. "Let's take this farther," she sighed as she took his hand and led him into one of the bedrooms.

* * * *

It was the most exciting and enticing hour that Matt could remember experiencing.

As he lay on his back next to Katie he could feel himself breathing heavily and could see and feel that she was doing the same. Above him Matt saw the slowly rotating ceiling fan cast it's shadow on them both as they laid on the backs on the bed covered below their waists in the dimly lit bedroom.

Katie finally sat herself up. "I'm going to see if anything worthwhile is in the fridge." She was magnificent to look at from Matt's perspective. Katie had creamy white skin stretched across her body. Not too thin, but certainly not heavy, Katie had all the right curves in all the right places from her smallish breasts to her near perfect derriere. As she walked from the bedroom Matt realized he wanted more of her.

Within seconds she returned with two cans of beer and a joint between her fingers. She tossed a beer at Matt and began to rummage through the night table searching for something.

"Do you have a match?" she finally asked. "I can't seem to find one."

"I'm afraid not," Matt replied. "I don't smoke."

She sighed as she rose from the bed again and left the room. In a minute she returned with the lighted marijuana joint between her lips.

She took a long drag and handed the joint to Matt.

Matt didn't take it. "Like I said, I don't smoke"

She smiled as she slowly let out the smoke. "I do smoke regular cigarettes, only these little things are different."

"I've had my share of marijuana in my time," Matt confessed. "But I swore off it long ago."

"Okay! Have it your way," Katie giggled. "Everyone here at school smokes these every day. It takes the pressure off."

Matt waved the cloud of smoke away from his face. "It also takes the reality away. It's not for me anymore. I've outgrown it."

"Well, I haven't," she shot back. "Do you mind?"

"No," Matt answered. "Just don't overdo it. I've seen guys at Temple get so out of it they didn't know what way was up."

"I can't get through a day without it," Katie told him as she took another drag. "Especially since my Mom died." She followed by swallowing a gulp of the beer which ran from the sides of the can down her chin and onto her breasts. "Oops! Sorry....I'm such a slob," she then giggled.

"You were high when you met me for pizza tonight," Matt realized.

She nodded. "Like I said, can't get through the day with it."

"So it wasn't my magnetic personality that made you want to sleep with me," Matt sighed as he lay on his back and stared at the ceiling fan. "It was the pot!"

Katie laughed, rolled over and straddled him, the joint still sticking out of her mouth. Suddenly the ashes fell from the smoke and landed on Matt's chest.

"Jesus!" Matt hollered as he brushed the burning ashes off him. "That's enough!" He took the stub of the joint from her mouth and put it in the ashtray on the night table.

Katie laughed and giggled as she rested herself onto his chest and kissed his neck. "I'm ready to go again," she whispered.

Matt complied with her wishes and wrapped her in his arms kissing and caressing her face and neck.

* * * *

As Matt stood at the bottom of the stairway leading down from the El platform at K&A he thought about his relationship with Katie and how it had progressed since their first date four weeks ago.

From the unexpected excitement on their first true date, their times together had taken on a more comfortable air. They now had a more normal relationship each time they met punctuated by explosive sexual encounters.

Katie had originally admitted knowing little about Philadelphia when she first met Matt. After two months exploring downtown and the area around Penn's campus she was ready to venture into Matt's neighborhood.

Katie had called Matt when she and her roommate Emily were about to leave their dorm and he approximated the amount of time, include El time, it would take to get to K&A. The girls were late, as usual.

Finally, he saw the girls descend down the stairs toward him.

Emily reached him first, gave him a bear hug and spun Matt around away from Katie, who was slowly coming down from the landing.

"High ya, Mister Matt!" Emily's voice echoed in the stairwell. "I missed you!"

From the unexpected excitement in her voice Matt guessed that Emily was already high.

Emily Lourdes was a Penn freshman just like Katie. She was from Hawaii and was a mix of European, Japanese and native Hawaiian. Her chocolate colored skin, almond shaped eyes and black hair disguised all her Caucasian genes. If you just heard her voice you would think she was a typical American teenager. But Emily was far from typical.

"So this is the famous K&A," Katie sneered as she looked at the intersection. She saw a flock of pigeons fly out from under the El as a train screeched into the station.

She saw the trolley car rolling up to the concrete island on Allegheny Avenue. She saw, heard and felt the rush of a truck passing by spewing a black cloud of exhaust fumes. "We have neighborhoods just like this in Chicago," she concluded.

"Well we don't have anything to match this in Honolulu," Emily added. "Looks like a neat place."

"So where are we headed?" Matt asked.

Emily handed him a piece of paper with the address.

"This isn't far from here," Matt told the girls. "Let's walk."

Within minutes they were ascending to the second floor of a grocery store on Kensington Avenue.

Immediately upon entering the apartment the group was blasted by loud music, a rush of warm air and overwhelmed by the acrid smell of marijuana mixed with a cloud of cigarette smoke.

Matt settled himself in a fairly comfortable chair next to a window. Before he sat down he cracked the window to let in some much needed fresh air. The girls had gone off to chat with some friends from school.

Matt had also noticed pairs cuddling together on the floor and on the couch that dominated the room. He also noted a pair of coeds dash by clothed in only a bra and panties.

He quickly decided that this wasn't going to be his kind of party. He had out grown the gassed up, drunken lifestyle. He was looking for more than that from life. He was content to sit in the sidelines and let his friends enjoy themselves as well.

In minutes he was joined by Emily, who had already shed her top and her jeans.

"How can you stand it?" she asked as she flopped down in his lap. "It's so hot in here!"

"I'm just fine, thanks," he told her as she snuggled up to Matt, nestling her head into his shoulder. "And please remember I'm with Katie."

"I'm with Katie, too," Emily whispered to Matt as she kissed his ear. "You know," Emily sighed. "Katie and I share everything, you know."

"That doesn't include me!" Matt said as Emily licked and nipped at his neck. He started to laugh.

A moment later Katie joined them in the living room. She also had stripped to her underwear. She frowned when she saw Emily perched on Matt's lap but joined the pair placing her body opposite Emily's on his lap too.

"You're barking up the wrong tree!" Katie said to her roommate. "He's mine."

Emily smiled and began to squirm free from the others.

The pair began to push against each other to get one of them off Matt's lap. Matt struggled to separate the girls and stop them from crushing him.

Finally, Emily broke free and stood up in front of the others.

"If that's the way it's going to be!" she shouted. "Screw you!"

"That's the way it's going to be," Katie insisted.

Emily drew a wide smile, unhooked her bra and tossed it at Katie. "This is yours too!" she coldly stated. "You can have it back!" With that she stormed off into the crowd.

"Sorry about that," Katie whispered as she snuggled up to him. She had beer on her breath and her hair smelled like pot. "I know this is not your thing, but humor me and Emmy for a little while. Then we'll go."

"Whatever you want, honey," Matt replied. "Whatever you want."

* * * *

On a quiet Sunday winter afternoon, as 1970 became 1971, Matt was relaxing in the living room of the apartment off campus. It had become a home away from home for him as his relationship with Katie began to settle in a near normal routine. At least on the weekends.

Most of the week Matt went to his office and went back to his childhood home in the evening. On Fridays he would meet Katie downtown after work and spent his nights either in her dorm room or in the apartment for the Chicagoans. Surprisingly, he seldom saw any of the Chicago upperclassmen who leased the place.

Matt had settled in with a cup of coffee and the Sunday paper trying to catch up on the rest of the world. The news of the world was depressing in the winter of 1971, just as it had been on 1970. The war in Vietnam chugged on. Unrest in the cities persisted and politicians ragged against anything they didn't like just like they always did.

Matt concluded as he read on that this was the reason he never looked at the newspapers. There just never seemed to be good things happening.

"Put that silly paper down and look at me!" Katie's voice echoed in the room from the entrance to their bedroom.

Matt lowered the paper and stared at his girlfriend. She was standing in the doorway in a grass skirt and a top made out of half coconuts held together with thin strings of fabric.

"We thought we'd surprise you today," Katie giggled as stood in doorway. A moment later Emily came giggling into the room dressed in the same outfit. The contrast was stunning between Katie's creamy white skin and Emily's equally creamy light brown skin.

Emily was carrying a cassette which she dropped into a boom box on a nearby dresser and Hawaiian music poured out.

"I brought these outfits and the music with me from Hawaii. I figured I'd use them at a Halloween party, but they never had one here on campus.

"Fits me pretty well, don't you think?" Katie said as she adjusted the coconuts covering her breasts. "Pays to have small tits like Emmy and me." She laughed as she adjusted Emily's coconuts as well.

"Absolutely!" Matt exclaimed. "Where'd you get these?"

Emily answered. "I used to work at a luau down in Hilo. Strictly for tourists. The closing number of the show was when all the girls came out wearing these. The men loved this. Their tongues were hanging out!"

The girls began to Hula dance to the music. Their swaying was almost in sync.

"She's pretty good for a mainlander," Emily said.

Katie asked. "What do you think, Matt?"

"I think this is quite a treat! What's next?"

The two girls stopped dancing and jumped on the couch with Matt. "This!" Emily laughed as she sat on his lap.

Katie pulled on Matt's arms until the three of them were soon rolling on the floor.

* * * *

Unfortunately for Matt and Katie, Emily began to hang out with them more and more. Sometimes she was a pleasure to be around with her wry sense of humor and her uncensored mouth, but other times she was a nuisance. Emily also added a sexual charge to everything around her and she had eyes for Matt to boot.

There was that one time when the girls showed up dressed like hula girls that Matt had given in. He soon regretted that day. He loved and wanted to be with Katie and her alone.

Matt was getting used to her pawing at him when he least expected it. He was getting used to Emily turning up at the least opportune moment in various stages of undress.

Matt was even embarrassed when the young girl turned up in his bed one morning, snuggling herself up to both him and Katie.

Katie had been patient throughout it all, but Matt could tell she was getting irritated by her roommate.

Matt concluded that the only way he was going to solve the Emily problem and allow him to concentrate his attention on Katie was to find someone else for Emily to turn her attention to.

He thought about Bob Finlay, Matt's close friend and occasional wingman. Bob had a winning personality and was probably better looking than Matt who hoped that was enough to overcome Emily's infatuation.

Matt had set up a double date for dinner. Again, he chose the pizza joint where he had first eaten with Katie. Again, the girls were late.

"I hope this girl is worth it," Bob commented as both men looked longingly toward the door to the restaurant. "Hope you're not wasting my time on some dog."

"Would I steer you wrong?" Matt asked back. "Believe me, she's a winner. Emily is a pretty little thing with a great sense of humor."

"That's a bad sign!" Bob shot back. "Great sense of humor is code for a dog. How else could you describe her?"

"Exotic."

"As in dancer?"

"No! Just take my word for it, she is something special."

Bob smiled. "That's another code word for dog."

Matt was saved from the rest of the conversation by the girls, who glided into the restaurant and into the booth next to the men.

"Hi!" Emily extended her hand to Bob. "I'm Emily and you must be Bob."

"Nice to meet you," Bob answered as he shook her hand. He was looking over the girl with an approving smile. Emily was wearing a pair of shorts and a plain white tee shirt. Her bronze skin glowed.

Katie sat across from Emily and was dressed in shorts and a halter top. "Bye the way, Bob, I'm Katie. Sorry my ape of a boyfriend didn't have the courtesy to introduce me."

"Time to order," Matt said as a waitress appeared at their table. "I'm starving!" He noticed that both Bob and Emily were looking the other over approving. He thought to himself that this may work out after all.

* * * *

Bob had to agree with Matt that Emily Lourdes was a catch. The petite Hawaiian was attractive. She seemed to be smiling all the time and warmed up to his own sharp personality. Bob felt they could have fun together if he could get the girl to stop looking longingly at his friend Matt.

The four of them left the restaurant quickly after finishing their pizza and it was only a short walk to their apartment off the Penn Campus. Matt had told Bob that the apartment wasn't the girl's, but they used it frequently.

Once inside Matt and Katie quickly vanished into a bedroom while Emily fetched a couple of beers from the kitchen.

"So what do you do?" Emily asked Bob as they settled next to each other on the sofa.

"I work construction," Bob answered.

"So…..no college?"

"No," Bob quickly answered. "Don't have the brains for it. Not like Matthew. He's one of the smartest guys I know. I'm just a working stiff from the neighborhood."

"College is so overrated!" Emily stated as she sipped the beer. "Way too much free time!"

"Matt used to tell me that college made him budget his time better," Bob said back. "When you're out there in the hot sun building houses you don't have a chance to budget your free time. You don't have any."

After the third beer the girl moved closer to Bob. She brought herself up to Bob's ear and whispered. "Want to fool around?" she asked.

Bob felt a little embarrassed but turned his head to face her and kissed her gently. "Sure," he whispered back

After a few minutes of groping Bob found his hand underneath her top and her hands were in his lap struggling with his belt and zipper.

"Aren't we moving a little too fast?" Bob softly spoke.

"Not too fast to me," Emily answered back as he withdrew her hands from his lap and pulled off her top. She leaned back on the couch and pulled him toward her. "Not too fast for me!" she repeated.

* * * *

When Bob woke up he felt the Emily's body next to his on the floor of the apartment's living room. Both were covered with a weathered Indian blanket and nothing else. She was still sleeping soundly as he tried to wiggle himself free of her embrace.

He did manage to bring her back from dreamland. "What's going on?" she asked as her head rose up from Bob's shoulder.

"Time to get up," he whispered.

"Nope!" she said back as she drew her lips to his and gave him a long and very affectionate kiss.

Bob heard giggling from across the room. He searched to find Katie sitting in an easy chair with her legs curled up under her. She was wearing Matt's button down dress shirt, totally unbuttoned and exposing the silhouette of her breasts as she turned to get up.

"We need to wrap this up," Katie told them. "The boys can't stay here overnight. Against the rules."

"Oh, yeah," Emily answered. "And we should get back to the dorm. I've got four ticki-marks against me as it is. Another and I'll face disciplinary actions."

"Okay, then! Get dressed!" Kate ordered. She stood up from the chair and grabbed pieces of Emily's and Bob's clothing and threw them at the pair.

Emily caught her tee shirt in mid-air as she stretched the last bit of sleepiness from her body. As she put the shirt on she asked Katie, "Do you have anything? I'm starting to come down."

Katie opened up the drawer of the table next to the chair and pulled out a pair of neatly wrapped joints and a lighter. She walked over to Emily and handed them over.

"Hey!" Matt called out from the bedroom. "I need my shirt if I'm to get going."

"I'm coming," Katie called to him as she turned toward his voice. As she walked she stripped off the shirt and tossed it into the bedroom.

She then turned to face Emily and Bob. "Tada!" she shouted as she posed for them in her panties and nothing else. She then turned and vanished into the bedroom.

"Shit! I wish I had that body of hers," Emily said softly as she watched her roommate disappear. It was true that Katie was half a foot taller than the Hawaiian girl and that her figure was a bit more filled out than Emily's, but Bob didn't feel Emily was any less attractive.

"Here," Emily said as she offered the smoke to Bob after lighting up and taking in a long drag.

"No thanks," Bob replied as he turned her hand away.

"Don't you do pot?" Emily asked as she drew in more from the smoke.

"Occasionally," he told her. "Kind of have to be in the mood."

She smiled. "I'm always in the mood. Most everyone I know is mostly in the mood all of the time. What we just did is so much better when I'm high."

"Like I said," Bob responded as he stood up and pulled up his pants. "I have to be in the mood."

Emily pouted. "Are you sure? You can have the whole other joint. Sex is so much better when you are really, really high."

Bob just shook his head and kept on dressing. "Maybe next time."

"Your loss," she smiled as she too finished dressing.

Within minutes the girls had kissed their men goodbye and started off toward their dorm. Bob and Matt started back toward 30th Street and the trip home.

"Man," Bob commented to Matt. "That was something! Is it like that all the time with those two."

"Much of it," Matt replied. "Especially if they are high or drunk."

Bob couldn't get the smile off his face as he thought about Emily. He hoped it hadn't been a one night stand.

* * * *

The phone call awakened Matt Michaels in the middle of the night. His cloudy eyes thought the time was after three AM. Matt lurched for the receiver so the ringing wouldn't wake up his mother. Matt had a separate line installed. But the loud ringer in his bedroom could wake the soundest sleeper.

"Yeah!" Matt mumbled as he struggled to consciousness. "Who is this?"

"Matt," a whimper of a voice came over the line. It was Katie.

"What's wrong?"

"I'm in jail," Katie's voice shook with each word. "Down in the 26th district. Can you come and bail me out?"

"What happened?" he asked.

"Can we talk about it later," Katie cried. "Please! Just please come and get me out of here!"

"I'm on my way," he assured her.

Matt dressed in a microsecond and he left the house without waking up his mom.

He raced down Kensington Avenue and Front Street. Both streets were covered by elevated trains and deserted at this time. Matt raced along trying not run too many traffic lights and reached the police station in record time.

An older police sergeant manned the front desk and smirked at Matt as he approached.

"Which one are you here for?" the gravelly voiced desk sergeant asked.

"Katie……Katherine Sherman," Matt stumbled over her name causing the sergeant's eyebrows to go up.

"You sure you know this girl?" the sergeant asked.

"Yes, she's my girlfriend."

"You don't look like a college student," the Sergeant stated coldly. "Or are you her dealer?"

"Dealer?" Matt questioned back.

"She was caught snorting coke when they were busted in the house," he said to Matt. "She didn't have any on her, but some lines were still on the table."

"Is she charged with anything?" Matt asked back. "What's her bail?"

The desk sergeant looked at his paperwork. "There are no charges! She wasn't holding so there is no charge of possession. Just take her home and get her cleaned up."

"How long will it take?" Matt asked.

"Where you going at 4AM? Got to catch a bus?"

Several minutes later Katie was brought up from holding cells. She looked pretty messed up with a pair of bloodshot eyes, her hands covered with dirt and her clothes disheveled. Streams of tears had formed rivers from her eyes and she looked very scared.

In the back of his mind Matt hoped that this would be a wakeup call for Katie. He hoped she might straighten out after this scare.

As soon as the policewoman let go of her arm she collapsed into Matt's arms. "I'm sorry," she wept softly as Matt wrapped his arm around and walked her out of the police station.

Once outside she broke free of Matt's grip and leaned against a nearby streetlight.

Matt went over to her and softly rubbed her shoulder. "You can rest here a minute then we can walk to my car. It's just across the street."

Katie began to laugh. "Man, that was great!" she shouted at the top of her voice. "Best high ever!!"

Matt realized that Katie had learned a lesson from her adventure. Maybe just the wrong lesson.

* * * *

"Things have been going better with Emily since she's gotten some of the wildness out of her system," Bob said to Matt as they drove downtown to meet the girls.

"How do you mean?" Matt asked as he cruised up Market Street toward Penn's Campus in his old grey and blue Chevy II.

"I've made her realize that you don't have to be stoned all the time," Bob continued. "She's just a kid, you know. This is the first time she's been out on her own. She's smart too, but not smart enough to learn from her mistakes yet. I figure I'm there to guide her."

"Are you getting infatuated with this girl?" Matt asked as he smiled back at his friend.

"I'm not falling in love with her, if that's what you mean," Bob answered as he rolled down the window and lit a cigarette. "Fact is, she's smarter and richer than me and not going to fall head over heels for a lousy fuckin' construction worker from K&A."

"That cutie is very impressionable," Matt said as he turned the car into a parking lot just past 36th and Market. "You clean her up and she just could fall in love with you. She's a real pretty girl but she's way out of your league, like you said. These are Penn co-eds, and they have both brains and money, but they are just teenagers suddenly deposited in a big bad city with time on their hands and money to burn."

"What about Katie?" Bob then asked.

"What about her," Matt said as he slid the Chevy into a parking space and turned off the engine.

"You're fucking around with her and she's just like the other one. I think she's hot as hell and has her eye out for you."

"She's worse than Emily," Matt went on. "Katie is pushing the limits. She's much different than the girl I first met on the train from New York. She's troubled by something, and I just can't pin down what it is."

"So where do we go from here?"

Matt lit up a smoke for himself and inhaled deeply. "Emily's just a kid and she'll follow along wherever you go with her. If it's the right direction you point her in, she'll be just fine. Katie is really no more mature, but she's trying to drag me into a direction I don't want to go, but I may be just too stupid not to follow that gorgeous little girl."

"You're no dope, Matt. You're falling for her."

"Damned straight."

* * * *

"I've got a real surprise for you tonight," Katie smiled to Matt as they sat on the bed. Each couple had migrated to their respective bedrooms after a night of watching two movies accompanied by snacks and beer. Matt's stomach felt queasy already and his head was spinning slightly from too many beers. Yet he was curious what Katie had in mind.

Katie had quickly slipped out of her jeans and tank top and already primed for her usual round a sex with Matt. He just stared at her beautiful body as she sat three feet away from him in her bra and panties and tried to remain unaroused.

Katie gave him a sideways glance. "Oh, no," she sighed. "You've got that look on your face like 'what is Katie going try tonight'!"

"Well, what is Katie going to try tonight?"

She jumped out of bed and took something out of the night table drawer. She then flopped down on the mattress and held a sugar cube between her fingers.

"Now, what's that?" Matt asked, knowing the answer.

"LSD," Katie looked curiously at him. "What else do you think it is?"

"Is it real?"

"I hope so! I paid way too much for the two cubes from a guy who sells on campus." The look on her face told Matt she was a little upset at him.

He explained. "You know, I've heard a lot about bad shit hitting the streets lately. Much of it is about false LSD, just like that there. It just makes people sick."

"My guy assured me it was real!" Katie shouted at him. "You going to try it with me or not?"

"I'll pass," Matt coldly stated.

"Your loss," she said as she popped the sugar cube in her mouth. She then bit down hard. As she chomped the cube with her teeth she said, "The guy told me it acts faster it you chew it rather than let it melt in your mouth."

When the cube was all gone, she just stared at her boyfriend.

"Well?" Matt said as he stared back at her.

"You going to get undressed so we can cuddle or are you going to make me go through this all alone?" she asked.

I think I'll just watch you," he told her. "Carefully."

Katie continued to stare at him and let out a deep sigh.

"Anything yet?"

Katie continued to stare off into space as she breathed harder. "Nope," she finally admitted. "Nothing!"

"You got robbed," Matt smiled back at her as he held back the urge to laugh.

"Got to give it more time," she went on. "They never said how long it would take."

Matt could no longer contain himself and burst out laughing.

"It's not funny!" Katie announced. "I'm so pissed at you right now! Stop making fun of me!"

"I can't help it," Matt said back. "You're acting like such a spoiled little kid right now because you can't get a high from a plain sugar cube."

"It's not just a plain sugar cube!" she screamed back at him. "I was assured…….Oh, Fuck you Matthew!"

She turned her back to him and stood up off the bed. She stood there for a moment swaying gently from side to side and then collapsed onto the floor.

* * * *

Katie's mind found her back in Chicago driving with her mother in the family car on the Ike from downtown toward their home just north of the city. It was a beautiful mid-summer's day and the expressway was crowded with cars.

Katie and her mom were shopping on Michigan Avenue for a new wardrobe for her freshman year at the University of Pennsylvania, the prestigious Ivy League school she had selected. Katie actually had the choice of several prestigious schools and her folks, fortunately, had the resources to send her anywhere she wished.

Her mom was personally unhappy with her daughter's choices.

"You could have gone someplace closer to home, dear," her mom was saying as the traffic began to ease ahead of them.

"Look, Mom," Katie argued back for millionth time. "I didn't want to go to a country campus. I'd be lost there. I didn't want Northwestern or any other Chicago school. What's wrong with an Ivy League school like Penn?"

"But it's so far away," her mother retorted. "We won't see you!"

"You won't be able to keep tabs on me! That's what you mean."

"Of course, that's what I mean!" her mom was getting agitated. "You weren't exactly the model student in high school, if you remember!"

Now Katie was getting hot. "Shit! Do you have to bring that up to me all the time. I drank a little. I partied a little. I made my fucking mistakes and learned from them!"

"Watch your mouth! And abortions cost a lot of money. I don't want to go through that again!"

"Jesus Christ!"

Mom screamed. "I said, watch your mouth!

"Stop bringing that up to me!" Katie shouted as she pounded the steering wheel with one hand. "I fucked up! I know it! I won't let that happen again."

"You want to be eight hundred miles away from Dad and I," her mom spoke softly and firmly. "That way you can be free to be the same little slut you were in high school."

Katie slammed the steering wheel again and pressed her foot on the accelerator. "You take that back!" she screamed as tears began to fall from her eyes. "Take it back!"

"I won't take it back!" her mom shot back. "You put your Dad and I through hell last year."

"I fucked up! I know it! How dare you call me a slut, you bitch!" Katie screamed as she swung her right hand in the air striking her mom in the shoulder. "You cheated on Dad, remember!"

"Little bitch!" her mom gritted her teeth and slapped Katie's face.

Katie angrily turned and faced her mother. "You're the bitch!"

"Watch out!" she heard her mom scream.

As Katie turned back toward the road she saw the rear of a delivery truck as her car quickly approached it.

She swerved!

The car's right side slammed into the back of the truck, bounced off and was swung around when it hit another car and finally stopped as it slammed into a guard rail.

The next thing Katie remembered was looking at her mother through the wreckage. Katie's face was covered with blood and her mother's motionless body was also bloodied.

She began to scream as she had that day as she came out of her nightmare.

* * * *

Emily heard Katie screaming from the other bedroom and shivers immediately ran up her spine. She quickly got out of bed, slipped on a tee shirt and ran toward the screaming.

She found her roommate sitting on the floor trembling in Matt's arms and screaming at the top of her lungs.

"What the hell did you do to her?" Emily frantically asked as she took the girl from Matt's arms and tried to sooth her by rocking her. The screaming subsided.

"I didn't do anything," Matt explained. "She took a sugar cube laced with LSD; I think. She collapsed on the floor and woke up screaming something about her mother."

Emily explained as she continued to hold and rock her friend. "She's had this nightmare before. She was driving a car back home and had an auto accident. Her mother died in the accident."

"She told me how her mom died in a traffic accident," Matt agreed. "But when she told me about this, she never mentioned that she was in the car."

Emily continued to rock Katie as Bob joined them in the bedroom. "Katie probably didn't mention it because she had blocked it out of her consciousness. She was driving the car when her mom was killed but those memories only come back to her when she dreams. She used to have nightmares about this when she first came to school. They stopped when she met you, Matt."

"Is she going to be alright?"

"What do you think?" Emily shot back. "Why do you think she goes on these binges? She can't face what happened, so she hides behind the booze, the drugs and the sex. Why do you think I'm always hanging around you guys? I'm frightened for her. I'm frightened for what she's doing to herself!"

"Then why haven't you ever said anything to me?" Matt asked.

"I thought she was better," the Hawaiian answered. "Today was a setback! I really thought she was better." She continued to cradle Katie in her arms as the girl started to come out of her stupor.

"What happened?" Katie mumbled to Emily.

"You had a bad dream," Emily explained. "Do you remember what you were dreaming about?"

"I guess it's about the accident," Katie mumbled. "What did I say this time?"

Matt answered. "You were screaming about the accident and your mother."

"I was back there again?" Katie mumbled, mostly to herself. "Was I at the accident scene?"

Emily answered. "You were there. Don't you remember?"

"No," Katie whispered. "I wasn't there. It wasn't my fault.

* * * *

Emily and Bob needed to get away from the craziness surrounding Katie Sherman. The pair had taken to the cool night air to enjoy each other's company and to speak more freely.

It had been two days since Katie's drug induced breakdown. She was finally acting normal and not haunted by her nightmares of the accident from last summer.

"It was amazing to watch you with Katie," Bob commented after a few minutes of walking along the grass lined sidewalks of Penn's campus.

"It was nothing," Emily said back as she smiled at her current beau. "You just have to stay calm and not get caught up in Katie's craziness."

"When I first met you," Bob continued, "I figured you as a spoiled teenager deposited in the city with little experience and little brains in her head. You were unbelievably cute but not much more than that. You amaze me with how in control and smart you actually are."

The pair sat on a nearby bench and Emily explained, "Most people, particularly boys, look at my exterior and never consider the person I am inside. I was number one in my class in Hawaii. I got a full ride to the University of Pennsylvania on my smarts and not my connections. I'm smart enough and quick enough to know when to show my intelligence and when to just show someone the exterior Emily. I'm not just a hula girl. Christ! I'm not even that pretty."

Bob smiled back at her. "You are pretty and smart, too. I'm just a guy from K&A who barely made it through high school and works construction building houses in the suburbs. You impress me."

She smiled back at him. "Don't underestimate yourself. You're smart enough to get by and not just in the academics but in life. Plus you're kind and considerate. You never tried to take unfair advantage of me and never treated me like I'm a dumb Hawaiian hula girl in a coconut top."

"Do you own one of those?"

"One of what?" she looked curiously Bob.

"A top made out of coconuts!"

"I actually do," Emily responded with a smile. "I'll have to try it on for you sometime. I used to dance part time at a luau restaurant and the finale included us stuffing our tits into coconuts halves and parading around in grass shirts. My tits were small enough to fit the top and it didn't bother me to dance around nearly naked. And the money was good."

Bob just shook his head. "Like I said, you amaze me Emily Lourdes."

She reached over and gave him a pecking kiss. "Let's start back. I'm getting cold."

They began walking hand in hand back to the apartment. Within minutes Emily spotted a solitary figure standing underneath a street lamp. She recognized the man immediately.

"See that guy over there," she whispered to Bob. "That's the guy Katie and I bought our weed from. I wonder if he sold her the bad dope."

Bob immediately changed direction and picked up his pace and started for the drug dealer.

"No. Bob!" Emily shouted as she began to follow him. "Stop! Don't do this!"

"Stay back, Em!" Bob called back to her. "Let me take care of this."

The drug dealer, a tall skinny man with a scrawny beard, just stood his ground a stared at the pair moving his way. There was no one else on the street.

"I want a word with you," Bob declared as he neared the man.

"You stay back mother fucker!" the man answered back in an angry voice. "I don't want no trouble, you hear!"

Bob stopped ten feet from the man. "You've been selling dope to these college kids. I want it to stop!"

"You ain't the boss of me!" the man shouted. "Get the fuck out of here before I get mad!"

"Just stop……" Bob began as he took another step toward the man.

The drug dealer drew a revolver out of his jacket pocket and pointed it at Bob. "You get back now! You hear! Get back!"

"Shit!" Emily cried. "He's got a gun!"

She took steps to close the distance between her and Bob.

"You're not going to use that!" Bob announced. "It'll draw too much attention."

"You are wrong," the man coldly stated as he pulled the trigger of his revolver and planted two bullets into Bob's chest.

Bob collapsed to his knees and then he hit the ground.

"Bobby!" Emily screamed as she knelt down beside him. When she looked up the black man was gone.

When she looked down, she saw no life in Bob's eyes.

"No, Bobby, no!" she cried as she held his body.

* * * *

Emily, Matt and Katie exited the funeral home on Allegheny Avenue in Matt and Bob's old neighborhood. All three of them knew they couldn't stomach going to the cemetery. All three of them knew they drew some of the responsibility for what happened to Bob. None more than Katie who was barely holding it together.

Instead they found a booth in the back of a small restaurant and stared blankly at the coffee cups until the coffee itself had grown cold.

Finally, Matt broke the silence.

"We've got to put this behind us and get on with our lives," he said to the women sitting across from him in the booth. Both girls were close to tears. "No more crazy parties or drinking and definitely no more drugs."

"I agree," Emily sobbed as streams of tears began to roll down her cheeks.

Katie just shook her head. "I don't know if I can do that. I've got such a craving right now. I need a hit so bad."

"You're coming down from all the crap you've been feeding your body," Matt told her. "You've got the DT's and it's going to get worse before it gets better."

Emily held her friend's hand. "I'll help you through it," she softly whispered to Katie. "We'll get through that and the grief together."

Katie was silent, just shaking her head, biting her lip and sobbing softly.

Matt reached over and clutched Katie's other hand. "Just hang in there Babe! It will get better."

"Who says it gets better?" Katie asked. "Right now it looks like one deep dark black hole."

"It will get better."

Katie still shook her head like she didn't believe him and quietly sobbed.

* * * *

Emily awoke two days later with the feeling that something was wrong. She was back in her dorm room for the first time in a week and was disoriented as she scanned the room. Finally, she realized exactly what was wrong. Her roommate Katie was not in her bed. As a matter of fact she was nowhere in the dorm room.

Emily quickly put on her robe and ran down the hall to the bathrooms. She searched the showers and each of the stalls, but Katie did not turn up.

She then ran across the floor to the common room where many of the coeds spent their free time. Katie wasn't there either.

"She's just gone!" Emily moaned was she ran back to her room to call for help.

She called Matt at the bank. She got a switchboard operator who could not locate him and decided she was wasting her time as the operator tried extension after extension to no avail. Whatever Matthew was doing she was not going to connect with him over the phone.

A crucial hour passed before she could get downtown to his office. She begged the receptionist on his floor to pull him out the meeting.

He was not pleased with Emily when he first saw her. "What's wrong, Em? It better be good because my bosses are getting damned impatient with me."

"She's gone, Matt!" Emily whispered. She was uncomfortable in the white collar computer office. She felt everyone was staring at the petite Hawaiian in dungarees and a Penn sweatshirt. Everyone around her was in suits or dresses.

"What do you mean she's gone?"

"I woke up this morning and Katie just wasn't there. She's nowhere on the dormitory floor or anywhere in the building," Emily explained. "I've got a bad feeling about this?"

"Okay! Here's what I need you to do," Matt's eyes revealed that he was thinking as he spoke. Emily felt he didn't know exactly what to do either. "You need to call the police and report her missing. You also need to talk to her dean to find out if the school knows more about her whereabouts than we do. You then need to wait for me to meet you at the dorm and we will look for her."

Emily mildly shook her head. He was giving her things to do just to keep her mind from thinking the worst.

"We'll figure it out, Emily," Matt clutched her shoulders tightly. "Stay calm and let's hope she turns up with some kind of excuse."

"She's gone searching for dope," Emily whispered to Matt.

"I know," he said back. "Let's just hope we can find her before she finds any."

* * * *

It took three days before Matt got a lead on Katie's whereabouts. She was leading a low-profile existence on Philly's streets and the police were less than enthusiastic about finding a single junkie in a town overrun with them.

Katie Sherman's father provided the first and only clue as to where she might be. Matt had contacted him to let him know how low Katie had sunk. Her father was unhappy with what had happened to his daughter and was now on his way to Philadelphia to find her and take her home. He had arranged to get her into a program once he got her back to Chicago. He held himself responsible for what Katie was going through. He realized he should have never allowed her to come to school after the accident with the truck.

Her father did discover she had used her credit card to buy some toiletry items at a downtown pharmacy and that was where Matt and Emily started their search for her.

It was nighttime before Matt & Emily began their search through the streets of Philadelphia, east of City Hall.

They hit the stores on Market Street before they closed and eventually wound up on Arch Street around midnight. As the air became colder the corners, alleyways and alcoves of Arch Street became more deserted although Matt could feel eyes looking at him and Emily from the darkness.

The only foot traffic came as the late show at the Troc let out onto Arch Street. A small crowd of overweight men emerged from the old burlesque house, now purely a strip joint, and wandered up toward Market Street's public transportation.

Matt decided to get more aggressive and began to show Katie's picture to every derelict and junkie he found in the dark hallows of the street. Each and every one of them shook their heads in denial and backed further into the darkness of their corner of the world.

"We'd better give it up for tonight," Emily pleaded with him. "It's too creepy out here."

"There's plenty of life going on in the hidden places around here," Matt assured her. "Katie's living on the streets and on the edge. This place is just the kind of place she'd be."

They continued up toward Broad Street and stopped in front of alleyway that contained a series of trash cans from restaurants inside the Reading Terminal Markets. Matt could hear the people in there rustling through the trash cans.

He and Emily walked side by side into the alleyway. Matt lit up his flashlight and the group of disheveled people quickly began to scatter. All except one obscured figure sitting on the ground in the corner past the trash cans.

"Katie!" Emily gasped as she recognized her friend. The girl was sitting on the cold ground in a torn pair of jeans and a tank top desperately trying to put a tie on her arm while holding a syringe in her mouth.

Both Matt and Emily were standing directly over the girl within seconds as Katie tried to stick the syringe into her vein. Emily grabbed her hand to stop her.

The women struggled over control of the heroin filled syringe while Matt stood by completely frozen.

"Matt! Help!" Emily called back to him as Katie started to get up.

"Leave me alone!" Katie shouted as she pushed Emily off her and against the adjacent trashcan, which spilled over on the alley.

Emily looked at her hand and realized she had the syringe.

"Give it back!" Katie shouted. "Give it back and get away from me!"

Matt finally shook himself back to reality and wrapped his arms around Katie. "Calm down, Katie," he told her. "We're going to get you some help!"

Katie struggled to free herself from his grip. "I don't want your help! Let me go!"

Emily threw the syringe toward the street as she took Katie's arms and examined the pin hole marks of other heroin injections. "Look what you're doing to yourself! You need help! Let us help you!"

Katie continued to struggle to free herself. "I don't want your help! I need you to leave me be!"

Somehow Katie managed to free herself from Matt's grip and staggered toward the syringe on the alleyway floor. Emily beat her to it and kicked the syringe into the street.

Katie ran toward it.

"Katie! No!" Emily shouted as the girl was out of her reach.

Matt began to run toward the girl as she reached the syringe and bent down to pick it up.

"It's broken, dammit!" Katie moaned as she looked at the syringe. "It's no good to me now."

She took two steps away from Matt. Katie stood there defiantly staring at him.

Matt saw headlights glowing from behind the girl.

"Katie!" Matt shouted. "Look out! Move!"

Instead, Katie slowly turned to the face the headlights.

As the headlights passed Katie disappeared for a moment and emerged from below the truck thirty feet down the street, a bloodied mess with the syringe still clutched in her hand.

Emily screamed.

The truck moved on away from the scene.

Matt and Emily ran up to Katie just as the broken syringe dropped from her hand.

"She's dead," Emily cried. "Oh, God……..she's dead!"

Matt felt for a pulse and had to agree. He reached over to her eyes, both wide with shock and empty of life and closed them with his hand.

"What'll we do?" Emily questioned as she sobbed.

Matt sat himself away from the girl he had loved so completely and passionately. "There's nothing we can do. Her nightmare is over."

Angela

The boardwalk was as crowded as Benny could ever remember. The sights, sounds and smells of the mid-August night surrounded Benny as he walked along, alone as his friends had now abandoned him. The people parading along the Ocean City boardwalk were the usual mix of the older people, younger pairs with kids tagging along or teenagers roaming in their usual packs. Quite different from the crowds he had experienced in Saigon just a few weeks before.

Benjamin Lefkowitz was none the worse for wear after his year in Vietnam. He had been stationed in Saigon repairing electronics for American installations in the city the whole time. He hadn't even set one foot into the jungles and only every so often heard the remote crackle of gunfire or the pop of explosives far away from where he was. Only a couple of times was Benny under any direct attack. Now, those nightmares still haunted him, but only briefly during his sleep.

Finally home and mustered out of the army, Benny was coaxed by his old high school friends to join them for a weekend down the shore.

Now, on the first night in, his pals had abandoned him to chase a pair of tube topped girls ahead on the boards.

Benny felt like a slice and a Coke instead.

He ordered from the pizza stand and was fumbling around for his money as the girl at the counter set the soda down in front of him.

"Here you go, Benny!" the girl stated in a slightly nasal voice.

He was still fumbling for change as he nodded absentmindedly.

"You don't remember me, do you?" the voice asked.

Benny looked up and saw a very familiar face. The same wide blue eyes, sandy colored hair and, as she smiled, a pair of world class dimples. He was embarrassed as he quickly looked down and put together the change to pay for his snack.

"Aren't you going to talk to me?" she asked.

Benny felt self-conscious as his old high school fear of Angela Antenucci surfaced from the recesses of his soul. He had known Angela since the seventh grade, and she always seemed to know his weaknesses. She and her girlfriends used to relentlessly taunt him and tease him in both Junior High and High School back in Kensington. Mostly they took advantage of his shyness and immaturity then and he wondered if those feelings were bubbling up to the surface again.

He knew though that he was a better man than he was a boy.

"You cut your hair," he stated flatly.

"Do you like it?" she asked as she smiled back at him and ran her fingers though the shortened pixie cut.

He quietly nodded.

"Come on, Benny!" she shot back at him, grinning from ear to ear as her dimples sparkled. "Don't you think you can get past high school."

His eyes turned up to meet hers. Angela had used her sharp tongue to torment him throughout his youth to make his life miserable. She was probably the prettiest girl in his class, but all he could remember was avoiding her and running away from Angela and her girlfriends every time their paths crossed.

Since he had failed to respond, Angela continued. "What are you doing here. Heard you were over in 'Nam."

His eyes rose to meet hers. "That's right," he finally spoke. "Just back. Getting a little R&R down at the shore."

"Great to see you again," she smiled back.

"What are you doing here?" he then asked her, growing a little more comfortable with each word.

"Family owns this place," she answered. "Just helping out during summer break."

A deep male voice echoed from the back of the stand. "Hey Angie! Orders up! Get movin'."

She turned toward the counter behind her and grabbed the slice of pizza off the shelf. "Aw, shut up!" she shouted to the back. "Keep your shirt on!"

"Take yours off!" was the response from the back of the store.

"Smart ass," she mumbled as turned back to Benny.

He smiled back at her.

"Look, Benny!" she stated as she handed him the slice and the soda. "Can't talk to you now. But you can find me on the beach tomorrow. Up front near the Eleventh Street entrance."

He stared at her suspiciously. "You sure?" he asked. "You're not just kidding around with me."

Her smile widened again as she looked at him. "I mean it. No tricks!"

"Okay," Benny nodded. "See you tomorrow," he answered as he turned and walked away.

* * * *

Benny took a spot along the railing and was just finishing his Coke when his friends returned.

"No luck?" Benny questioned. He already knew the answer. If his buddies had come close to enticing the two girls in the white tube tops they wouldn't be back so soon.

They both shook their heads.

Dean Kusic and Paul McMahon were old High School pals of Benny's. Both had been untouched by the draft and so had remained in Kensington. Both worked for their fathers in their mom-and-pop business. Dean was set to become a plumber. Paul's family refurbished cabinets and such. Both had failed to grow up since graduation, even though it had been four years, so every weekend they headed for the shore, buying their beer in Somers Point before moving on to Paul's family place in the dry town of Ocean City.

On this weekend Benny had joined him. The beach and boardwalk were among of the few things Benny had missed in his stint in the service. He loved to walk the boards, shuffling through the crowds and listening to the sounds of the surf and the screeching of the seagulls. He loved the beach where he could sink his toes into the cool, damp sand near the water's edge and admire the girls in their bathing suits. Benny knew he would soon have to buckle down, get a job and move on. This may be his last chance to enjoy the beach and boardwalk scene.

"At least we tried," Dean shrugged his shoulders. Then he smiled. "There's always more tail to chase down here."

"Yeah," Paul chimed in. "Did better than you! Got a chance to look at a couple a prime piece of ass for a few minutes."

Benny just smiled.

"What did you do while we were gone?" Paul asked.

Benny still smiled. "Got a slice and a Coke. And ran into a girl I knew from the neighborhood."

Dean snapped back. "And who was that, pray tell?"

"She was working at a pizza stand down a block or so," Benny answered. "It was good catching up."

"Do we know her?"

"Yes," Benny answered. "Angela Antenucci."

Dean laughed. "So, how fast did you run away."

"I didn't," Benny answered back quickly. "I actually talked to her and she seemed pretty nice."

"You used to run and hide every time she came near you back at school," Dean went on. "I remember the time she ambushed you in the cafeteria. She'd rag on you like crazy! All you'd do was turn red and try to hide."

"Yeah," Benny conceded. "I was too shy back then."

"You were scared shitless!" Paul stated laughingly.

Benny could only nod knowing he was right.

"How'd she look?" Dean asked. "She changed much?"

"She's still really pretty," Benny answered. "Looks real good."

Paul interjected. "I'd steer clear of her if I were you."

"Why?"

"Rumor has it that she was connected to the Antenucci mob family from South Philly," Paul told him.

Benny disagreed. "First off, she's from Kensington, not South Philly. Secondly, she wouldn't be working at a pizza stand on a hot night in Ocean City if she were that well connected. Thirdly, she never struck me that way."

"How could you tell," Paul laughed. "You were always running away from her."

"She's Italian," Dean said next. "They are all kind of mixed up with the mob, aren't they."

"And all Pollacks are stupid, and all Jewish boys grow up to be doctors," Benny refuted him. "Stop stereotyping her. I would not want to be stereotyped and neither do you guys. There were plenty of Italians in our class and they weren't all connected to the Mafia."

Dean smacked his lips. "Boy I'd like to get a chance at her. Great bod! Nice tits! Could fuck that all day!"

"Grow up!" Benny rebuffed his friend. "You are all talk! You'd stand as good a chance with Angela Antenucci as…."

"As you do, Jew Boy!" Dean chided back.

Benny just smiled. "We will see," he mumbled under his breath. "I'm going to find her on the beach tomorrow, so we'll see."

* * * *

Benny got to the beach early and found it already crowded with multicolored umbrellas, families, teenagers playing with baseballs, soccer balls, footballs, and Frisbees, and lots of young girls in bikinis tanning themselves in the morning sun.

He soon realized that finding one girl on the crowded beach as akin to finding a needle in the haystack.

Yet, there she was! She was close to the surf sitting in a sand chair, seemingly asleep, in a bright white and red bikini. And she was absolutely gorgeous. Her tanned body seemed to glisten with beads of water sprayed up from the surf. Her face was serene as she lay there seemingly asleep.

Benny hesitated, thought about quietly leaving as he self-consciously stared at the scantily clad girl, but finally stood between the sun and her and watched as her eyes slowly opened.

"You know," he said to her. "You should never fall asleep on the beach. Especially alone. You'll wake up looking like a lobster."

Angela shielded her eyes with her hand and squinted back at him. "I'm not alone," she answered. "My girlfriends are right here."

"What girlfriends?"

She looked from side to side at two empty sand chairs and realized she was sitting alone. "Now where the hell did those girls go?"

"Then I'm glad I'm here," Benny smiled.

"They must have gone in the water," Angela waved. "Well, pull up a chair!"

Benny sat himself on the damp sand instead. "I bet you never expected me to show up this morning."

"I didn't know what to expect," Angela answered. "It seemed that you've overcome your shyness that I remembered, but I couldn't be sure."

"I kinda grew up," Benny answered. "A stint in the service will do that for you."

"That's not all it fixed," she smiled. "I don't remember you as being so muscular. You look very good now – handsome - not that you weren't nice looking back then."

"Oh really!" he laughed. "Then why'd you make my life so miserable in school."

She smiled broadly. "I don't really know. You just were an easy target. It was so simple to get you nervous and upset. The fact is most of us thought you were kind of cute back then. Now you are more than cute."

Benny was embarrassed. "Thanks," he managed to whisper.

"So what did you think of me back in school?" she asked.

"Well," Benny answered knowing he was treading on a touchy subject. "You were always very pretty, but you were mean to me all the time. I think we had more words right here and now than we ever had back in school. I was too petrified to talk to you then like I am now."

Her hand reached out an touched his arm. "I'm sorry for what we did back then. I guess I was mean to you……. for years!"

"Thanks," Benny liked the feel of her hand squeezing his forearm. "And I apologize for the way I always acted. Strange to think that now, here I am sitting next to the beautiful Angela Antenucci on a beach at the Jersey shore.

"Aw," her face turned away, "Aren't you sweet."

"And a nearly naked Angela Antenucci at that!"

She laughed, stood up and grabbed his hand. "Let's go get wet!" she said as she pulled him up off the ground and ran toward the surf.

Benny stood up too, took off his T-shirt, and ran after her into the ocean.

She stopped when the water was up to her shoulders. Once Benny caught up she reached out and wrapped her arms and her body around him.

"Now," she whispered. "Isn't this nice."

She pressed herself against Benny and tightened her grip on him. She hoisted her legs up and curled them around his torso. All the while the surf lapped both his and her body forming bubbles of salt water on them.

"Now what's this all about?" he asked.

She pressed her face toward his. "Oh, shut up! Shut up and kiss me," she said as closed her eyes and pressed her lips to his.

* * * *

It was near midnight when Benny ventured back to the boards. The crowds had mostly drifted off toward home by then and the boardwalk seemed lonely and quiet. The evening mist from the surf had crept up to the boardwalk and everything glistened against the yellow lights that lined the wooden walkway.

Benny had come up at this late hour to meet Angela after the stand where she worked closed up for the night.

As he leaned on the metal railing at the far side of the boardwalk across from the pizza stand, he saw her come out the side door to the shop, spot him, and start walking his way.

She was smiling that big broad grin of hers, dimples and all, as she walked toward him in a white cut off t-shirt and short shorts.

When she reached him she stretched up and kissed him lightly on the cheek.

"You smell like a pepperoni pizza," Benny stated as they parted. "One of my favorites."

She laughed. "I reek like a grease trap! I feel like I've just come out of the oven myself."

"I was trying to be kind," Benny answered back.

She grabbed his hand and began pulling him away from the railing. "I need to get home and change. I'm not spending the rest of the night stinking up the world."

They silently walked to the condo she rented with her two girlfriends on Ocean Avenue. It was right behind one of the amusement areas and the rollercoaster was still running there, the occupants screaming as the coaster plummeted from the apex of the ride.

They stepped into the darkened ground floor apartment and Benny realized that the other girls must still be out on the town.

Angela flipped on a lamp. "I'll be right back," she told him as she stripped off her top and began to walk toward the bedrooms. "Make yourself comfortable."

Within minutes she returned wearing sweats. She went into the kitchen, opened the fridge and pulled out a couple of beers before flopping down on the couch next to Benny.

"Boy! I'm really pooped!" she sighed as she handed one bottle to him. "I'm getting too old for this! Can't burn the candle at both ends."

"Too old!" Benny remarked. He looked her over. She was tired, but still looked great. "What are you, 22, just like me?"

"I was on the beach all morning and afternoon and then put in a full shift on my feet at the pizza stand," she answered as she sipped her beer. "Knocks the shit out of you!"

"Then why do it? I'd think you'd find a career by now."

She smiled. "It's a family business. We all have to pay our dues. The family paid for college. I agreed to work the pizza stand in return."

"Shouldn't you be through college by now."

"I took a couple of years off to find myself," Angela answered as she brushed her hair with her hand. "I'm going to nursing school back in Philly. A real career as you said." She smelled the hand that had just gone through her hair. "God! I still smell like pizza! I should shower."

"Great profession, nursing," Benny said. "Your parents should be proud."

"Actually not!" she laughed. "My mom just wants me to get married and give her grandchildren. My father wanted me to work the family business forever."

"Pizza stand waitress forever!" Benny laughed with her. "Not much of a future in that."

"That's not really the family business," she stopped laughing and smiling. "I know you've been away in the service, but you must have heard of the Antenucci family."

"From South Philly?"

"Yes."

"But we were in school together for six years," Benny said. "You're from my neighborhood. Not South Philly."

"My mom moved up with me to Kensington to get away from the family. She didn't want me mixed up in it."

"So what happened?" Benny asked. "Why do you seemed so involved in it now."

"My father paid for school even though Mom left him. Kind of obligated me to the family." She continued to sip at her beer.

"How long does this obligation last?" Benny asked.

"Forever."

"So what does a pretty young girl do for the Antenucci Crime Family?" Benny asked. "Become a hired assassin?"

"Jeez! You make it sound like a 1930's gangster movie," Angela shot back. "It's really more like a business than you can imagine. We own three stands like the one I'm at down here in OC. We have several restaurants in Philly and other businesses too."

"So what about all the stories you hear in the papers?"

"Oh, that's true too," she answered as she got up and walked toward the refrigerator. "We also run numbers in the neighborhoods and do some not so legit wholesaling. The legitimate businesses are places to run the not so legit money through." She reached in the fridge and got another beer. "It's more complicated than you think. You want another?"

"I'm good," Benny answered as he finished the one he had. He wasn't much of a drinker, and one was enough for the night.

"Why are you telling me all this?" Benny asked. "I thought the workings of organized crime would be secret."

"I'm not telling you anything you wouldn't know from reading the local papers," she answered as she stood over him. "It's not so secret as you might suspect. Anyway, you not a Fed, are you?"

Benny shook his head.

"Then it doesn't really count what I say," she smiled and quickly finished her second beer.

She flopped down next to him on the couch. "Okay," she began. "I've told you a lot about what I'm into. What about Benny Lefkowitz?"

"I haven't figured it all out yet either," he began. "I'm just a couple of weeks out of the army and don't know what I'm going to do from here. Probably go back to school and finish up. I'd like to build up on what I learned in the service; Computers, that kind of stuff."

"Computers! Wave of the future," she stated with the smile returning to her face. "Or so they tell me."

"Nothing wrong with nursing," Benny countered. "Very humanitarian."

"Enough praising each other's choices," she said as she stretched and yawned. "I'm too tired to talk!"

"Then maybe I should go." Benny got up off the couch.

She looked longingly up at him. "Thought maybe you'd like to stay." She extended her hand to him, and he pulled her up from the couch.

She then wouldn't let go of his hand instead pressing herself against him. "Wouldn't you like to know what I've got on under these sweats?"

"I'm game."

"Nothing," she whispered in his ear as she began to pull him toward the bedrooms. "Absolutely nothing!"

* * * *

Just three months earlier Benny was in Saigon, walking home with his crew after a long day of repairing equipment in the Embassy. Not unlike most other days the weather was hot and humid, with a cloudless sky and no breeze.

Benny and his fellow workers were dripping with sweat after only walking a brief distance.

Corporal Lenora Manning, the newest and only female on the repair team, was the first to complain. "Man! It's hot. We should have left the test equipment back at the Embassy." She struggled as she adjusted her gear.

PFC Willie Macon, a muscular black man from Chicago, went over to help and took the heaviest piece she was hauling off her hands.

"Willie, why are you doing that?" Technical Sergeant Tom Ianelli from New York, the detail commander, shouted at his subordinate. "She has to carry her weight just like all of us."

"I know that Sarge," the man responded. "But she's such a little thing. Needs a man's help."

Sergeant Benjamin Lefkowitz, the final member of the team, just smiled and continued ahead of the rest hauling his fifty plus pounds of gear.

"Come on, Willie!" Ianelli shot back. "You just want to get into her pants."

"Not much chance of that," Manning answered.

"Let's just quicken the pace," Ianelli told his crew. "Let's get back to base and cool off."

Benny, had outpaced the others and was twenty yards away. "Come on, guys!" he turned and shouted back at them. "Stop bickering and let's get a move on!"

Beyond the others in the group Benny spotted a white van speeding toward them and the crowded market they were passing. He instinctively knew what the van was up to.

"Move off the street!" he shouted back at the group as he himself moved away from the market.

Ianelli moved instinctively the same way as Benny, but Manning and Macon froze in the middle of the street.

Just as the van swerved and turned headlong into the market, Macon shielded Manning from what was coming.

The van exploded into a bright yellow and red flash followed by an expanded cloud of dense smoke which enveloped Macon and Manning.

The shock from the blast knocked Benny off his feet!

"Damned!" Benny shouted as he struggled to get his gear off himself and stumble back to his feet. He barely heard himself speak as his ears began to ring and the smoke now enveloped him.

Finally, the smoke began to clear and he moved slowly toward his comrades.

He heard the screaming from Lenora Manning above the other screams surrounding him as he neared her. She was mostly under Macon's body, her head and arms exposed and cut up. Macon, on the other hand was limp on top of her, his back ripped wide open from the cascade of shrapnel.

Benny knelt once he reached the pair and pushed Macon's body off of the woman. Despite the cuts on her frightened face, Benny could see she was also very angry.

"That was a damned fool thing to do!" she grunted as she up righted herself. She spun around and finally looked into Macon's eyes. She quickly realized the man was dead.

"Dammit, Willie!" she cried. "Why'd you think you had to protect me?"

"Because if he didn't, you'd be dead," Benny answered quietly.

Manning sat up and stared off into space. She began to sob uncontrollably.

* * * *

"Ben! Wake up! Wake up, please!" Benny heard Angela's voice awaken him from his nightmare.

He opened his eyes and came back to reality. He had broken out in a cold sweat and was shaking. "What? Where?" was all he could mutter.

"Jeez!" Angela moaned. "That was fucking scary. All of the sudden you became restless and began to shout in your sleep."

Benny began to realize he was in bed next to Angela. Both of them were naked and the bedroom was cold and dark. He lay on his back with the beautiful girl hovering above him, a look of dread and concern on her face.

It had been several weeks since he had started dating the girl. With both back in the neighborhood he had begun by picking her up after nursing school and spending more and more time with her as time passed. Now, he seldom went back to his old apartment and spent most of his nights with Angela.

Slowly, his senses began to come back to him, and he realized it was just the usual nightmare. His body began to cool down and his breathing was returning to normal.

"You got a smoke?" he asked.

She looked curiously at him. "You don't smoke," she told him.

"Sometimes I do."

She reached behind her and took out a pack of Parliaments from her night table drawer and handed it to him. She stroked his hair as he took out a cigarette and lit a match. His hands were still shaking, and he couldn't steady himself to light the smoke. As the match burned out she took both the cigarette and the matches, lit the smoke and handed it back to him.

"There," she said quietly as she put the matches and cigarettes back in her night table. "You were really spooked this time."

"Have I done this before?" Benny asked.

"Yes," she answered. "But you had always just muttered as you slept. This time you shouted and were moving violently in the bed."

"Sorry about that, Angie," Benny apologized. "I thought I had it under control until now.

She just shook her head, leaned down and kissed him gently. "It'll pass in time," she said. "You just got back."

"Hasn't passed yet! As you can see."

Angela lay down on top of him, her head on his chest. "Who are Manning and Macon?" she softly asked.

Benny placed a hand on her head and stroked her short blonde hair. "A couple of guys in my outfit," he explained. "Macon got it on the car bombing near the Embassy. The incident I keep replaying in my head."

"And Manning?"

"She survived because Macon shielded her from the explosion," he explained.

"You weren't hurt?" Angela asked.

"Not a scratch," he answered.

"What happened to Manning?" she asked. "Is he okay?"

Benny took one last long drag from the cigarette. "He's a she. Nice young girl from down south. She never got over it. She put a bullet into her own head five weeks later."

* * * *

They had gotten themselves into a comfortable routine as time went on. Angela was on second shift doing her rotations at Northeast hospital. Benny, who had recently begun his new job in downtown Philly, would pick her up after work and the pair would grab a late snack and coffee at the nearby diner on Aramingo.

Their routine seldom changed, and it had gotten to the point where they sat in the same booth every night. They knew the wait staff by name and vice versa. The servers even knew what Angie and Ben ordered each night.

"The usual?" Sandy the waitress asked, order pad and pencil at the ready.

"Yep!" Angela answered, not even looking at the menu.

Benny was looking closely at a page in the menu, which contained almost anything anyone would think of ordering. "I'm still thinking." Benny said softly.

"Just get him the usual," Angie told the girl.

"Not so fast," Benny went on. "Not so fast." He then closed the menu. "Two eggs over easy, hashbrowns and rye toast."

Angela smiled at Sandy. "Like I said! The usual."

As Sandy left their booth to place the order, Benny asked, "How'd it go tonight?"

Angela flashed a faint smile at him. "Not so interesting. Bed pan duty all night. They must have served the geriatrics something bad for dinner. They were crapping all over the place."

Suddenly, a man slipped into the booth next to Angie. She gave him room but did not look pleased. He was a thin man in his mid-twenties with unkept long black hair. He was dressed in a leather jacket looking to all the world like a biker.

"What the fuck are you doing here?" Angie stared at the man with the look of both distain and recognition.

The man sneered at her and slid her coffee cup over toward himself.

He took a gulp of coffee. "So, Sis?" he questioned. "Who's this guy."

"I'm Benny Lefkowitz," Benny answered. "Who are you?"

Angie answered instead. "This is my brother, Michael," she answered. "He's not supposed to be here."

Two other men slipped into the booth behind Angela and Benny. They looked as unsavory as her brother.

"We need to talk, Ange," Michael said as the food arrived. He grabbed Benny's platter and quickly dug a fork into the eggs. "Tell Jew boy here to take a walk."

"Don't make a scene here, Michael," Angela pleaded. "It's not the place or the time."

Michael was gobbling down Benny's meal quickly. Between bites he said, "Pop wants to see you. Tomorrow!"

"I'm working tomorrow."

"Pop calls," Michael shot back. "You come!"

"I'll think about it," Angie smiled back at him.

Michael finished Benny's egg breakfast for dinner in record time. "Pop says you come home to see him tomorrow. He ain't kidding."

Angela just stared at him as he stood up to leave.

"Thanks for breakfast, Jew boy!" Michael sneered as he began to leave. "See you around."

As Michael and his two cronies quickly left the diner Angie let out a deep sigh.

Benny reached out and took her hand. "Are you okay?"

Angela seemed to be holding back a tear. "Yeah, I'm okay. Sorry you had to deal with that."

"No problem," Benny answered.

Sandy suddenly appeared at their table.

"You want a reorder of your breakfast?" she asked.

"I've lost my appetite," Benny answered. "Just the check."

Sandy ripped up the check she was holding. "It's on the house," she said as she walked away.

* * * *

A few minutes later Angela and Benny emerged from the diner hand in hand and proceeded to his car.

"Oh, shit!" Angie exclaimed as she saw Michael and his two cohorts leaning against Benny's beat up old Dodge Dart.

Michael walked over toward the pair. "Thought we'd have a conversation with your kike boyfriend."

"Michael, please!" Angie pleaded as she let go of Benny's hand and placed herself between Benny and her brother. "Not here! Not now!"

"I can handle this," Benny stated coldly even though he knew he really was no match for the trio of South Philly hoods.

"No, you can't!" Angie hollered as Michael wrapped his arms around her and pulled her out of the way.

Within seconds Michael's henchmen were on Benny, pelting him with blows to his stomach.

Benny stumbled to the ground unable to catch his breath and was further pummeled by the hoods.

"Benny!" he heard Angie scream as she struggled to unwrap herself from her brother.

The pair of hoods gave Benny two swift kicks in the side before dropping away from the stricken man just as Angela succeeded to free herself and ran toward the fight.

Instinctively one of Michael's henchmen punched her in the face as she neared him, sending her to the ground.

As Angie struggled to get up and Benny lay writhing in pain on the ground, he heard shouting from the diner.

"I've called the cops!"

"You guys get out of here!"

He heard the faint cry of a police siren in the distance.

"Let's go boys!" Benny heard Michael's voice. He then saw the man leaning over him. "You stay away from my sister, Jew boy! This was only a taste of what you'll get!"

Benny then watched as he went over to Angie, still dazed and trying to right herself. "Sorry, Sis!" Michael said, not trying to help her at all. "You'd better show for Pop tomorrow, or I'll come back and really finish off your Jew boyfriend." Michael and his two friends disappeared into the darkness.

Angie crawled her way over to Benny and tried to comfort him. "I'm sorry," she cried as she stroked his hair and squeezed his arm. "I'm so sorry."

* * * *

The next morning, promptly at 10 o'clock, Angela knocked on the door to her family's rowhouse in South Philly. Her heart was pounding as she did so. It blotted out the pain she felt in her black and blue cheek from the blow she took to her face the previous night.

The door opened quickly and the man standing in the doorway waved her inside.

Sitting in his big recliner that dominated the dimly lit room was he father, Salvatore 'The Kingpin' Antenucci. He was a rapidly aging man of 62, his weight cementing him to his laz-z-boy, with green steel eyes and salt and pepper hair.

He waved for his daughter to take a seat, but Angela stood in front of him unmoving.

"I hear you got a new boyfriend," her father started in his gravelly voice. "Congratulations! But I hear he's also a Jew. Too bad!"

"My private life is my business," Angela defiantly answered. "You gave up the right to criticize my decisions when you threw Mom and I out of this house."

"We'll see," he shot back. "I'll decide what is my business and what's not."

"What is it that you really want, Pop?"

"Okay, I'll be blunt!" he answered her back. "This business of ours is a family firm. You are part of the family and I thought you'd come to your senses by now and agree to come back to the family."

"Not a chance," was Angie's answer.

"I'd think that over if I were you," he continued. "The K&A boys are our blood enemies, and they know you are living in their neighborhood. I'm worried they'll go after you to get to me. Or they may use your new boyfriend as bait."

"I'm not part of the family anymore," she interrupted him. "Other than working off my college debt we have nothing to do with you."

"The K&A boys may think otherwise." He told her. "Look, Angie, you're still my kid and I don't want anything bad to happen to you. You're also a lot smarter than your brother. You should be running the business by now. I don't want to be boxed into a corner between you and Michael. Come home! Work with me to put down this war between us and the K&A boys. I'm too old and sick for this shit!"

"I'm not coming back, Pop," Angie answered him. "I have a life of my own. A future! No matter what you say I'm not coming back."

Her father nodded his head. "Okay, Angie, have it your way. I'll do what I can to keep you out of this, but there's no guarantee. Be careful!"

Angela turned and quietly left the house.

* * * *

Angela Antenucci knew she was falling in love with this guy. He was warm and funny. He was fairly good looking and did not hold against her the fact that she harassed the crap out of him in school.

Benny Lefkowitz was not the most adept lover, but he tried hard. Angela found that he best enjoyed and performed when she straddled him and did most of the work when they had sex. Angie was convinced that he just loved watching her rhythmically move on top of him. He'd reach up and caress her breasts, small though they were, hardening her nipples and smiling as she reacted to his touch.

She enjoyed it as well, enhancing the experience as she quietly moaned during sex and ran her hands through her hair and along her body. Angie enjoyed watching his expressions as she slowly brought both of them to climax.

She would then collapse onto his chest and match her heavy breathing with his as he softly caressed her.

"You're really something else," Benny told her. "Really something great!"

"Sush!" she sighed as she hugged his torso.

"Never thought I'd be in sleeping with Angela Antenucci," Benny said, his breathing still heavy causing his chest and her body to pulsate up and down. "I'd never thought someone like Angela Antenucci would be naked with someone like me."

Angie propped her head up on her arms, folded together on his chest. "First off. You are a catch. You are sincere. You are somewhat pleasing to look at…."

Benny interrupted. "So are you…."

"Shut up!" she interrupted back. "You're smart. You're kind to people and animals. In short, you are a nice guy."

"Thank you," Benny smiled as he jumped back in.

"But you've got to stop calling me 'Angela Antenucci' like I'm some kind of prize or art object you've won," she concluded.

"But you are a prize," Benny answered. "First prize, I might add."

"Shut up!" she tapped her fingers into his chest. "Stop objectifying me! I'm a person, not first prize in some kind of contest."

He laughed. "I just can't wait to show you off to my friends. They'd all be standing there with their tongues hanging out to know that I am with Angela Antenucci."

"There you go again," she spat back at him. "Stop it!" She began to lift herself off him and off the bathroom floor where they had just had sex.

"Where are you going?" he asked.

"I'm not going to lay here and be treated like a piece of ass."

"But you are!" Benny laughed. "And a fine piece of ass, I might add."

She stood up and gave him a sour look as she wrapped herself in her robe. She threw a second terry robe down on top of him. "Here! Put this on. The excitement's over."

When both were fully robed she opened the door and stepped out of the bathroom. Her roommate Linda was waiting there anxiously with a disgusted look on her face.

"It's about time you two finished up in there," her roommate said sarcastically. "I was about to bang on the door. I need to pee."

Linda rushed by them and slammed the bathroom door closed behind her. "Don't think I don't know what you two were doing in here, either," she called through the door. "You two were not as quiet as you'd like to believe."

"Sorry!" Benny answered the closed door.

"Don't be sorry," Angie told him. "There were plenty of times she was just as loud while she was banging one of her boyfriends."

"Hey!" they both heard through the door.

"How about the time I walked into the apartment and found you and some guy going hot and heavy on the couch?" Angela giggled as she talked. "What was that guys name? Stan or something."

"Stephen," Linda replied through the closed door. "And he was only a one-night stand! You and Benny-boy are doing this every night!"

"You are jealous," Angie smiled as she talked to the closed door.

"Dammed straight I'm jealous!" Linda stated as she reopened the bathroom door. "I haven't had a consistent boyfriend in two years."

"Just one-night stands!" Angie shot back.

Linda smiled. "Yeah, just one-night stands!"

Angie turned to Benny. "Should we accommodate her?" she asked.

Benny smiled at her and then turned to Linda. She was a short and very thin girl he had also known for years from school. She was pretty enough with her dark eyes and dark hair, but she was no Angela Antenucci.

"Fuck off!" Linda finally said. "You're looking at me like you're picturing me naked!"

Benny self-consciously turned his head away.

"Oh, well! I don't do threesomes!" Linda snapped.

"Neither do we!" Angie snapped back.

"Let me think about that," Benny smiled as he said it.

"Fuck you!" both girls said in unison.

* * * *

Linda Murray liked being Angela Antenucci's roommate. She liked it even better when Angela was working a double shift and Linda had the apartment all to herself. She liked the solitude of the empty apartment so that Linda could read a book, take a long bath, or just sit around enjoying the quiet. All too often their apartment was crowded with the two girls and at least one male partner, short term or long term.

Mostly it was Linda's one-nighters that found their way into the apartment, usually sprawled out on the living room couch or on the carpeted floor. Until Benny, Angela's bedmates were few and far between. Now, Linda realized, Benny Lefkowitz was in Angela's life to stay so she had to make allowances.

But Benny and Angie had an interesting relationship, Linda had to admit, consistently peppered with loud words, punctuated by door slams and an occasional pot thrown across the room.

Tonight, finally alone, Linda had the luxury of a hot bath, just finished, a long glass of red wine and a steamy mystery novel to indulge in. She sunk into the soft cushions of the couch and wrapped her legs under the terry robe as she took the first sip of wine.

Just as she opened the first page of her novel the doorbell rang. Linda sighed, wondering who was disturbing her peace, put down the book and went to the door.

Through the door she called. "Who's there?"

"Police." A hardened voice said back.

Linda looked through the peep hole. "Show me your badge," she stated.

After examining the badge as best she could through the peep hole, Linda finally opened the door.

"Detective Russo," the man stated as he entered the apartment.

His partner lingered back at the doorway entrance and did not speak.

Russo continued. "We're looking for Angela Antenucci."

"She's not here," Linda answered as she felt a chill and wrapped her arms in front of her.

"Who are you?" he then asked her.

"Linda Murray," she answered. "And it's really none of your business."

"Do you know where Antenucci is or when she'll be back?"

"No," Linda flatly stated as she backed further and further into her apartment. She felt threatened by the cops. One never moved from the doorway, but the other man, Russo, kept moving closer to her.

"What has she done?" Linda nervously asked.

"Who said she has done anything," Russo said back.

"I assumed……"

"Don't assume, Ma'am," the detective said as he picked up Linda's glass from the end table and sniffed her wine. "We're just curious as to her whereabouts."

"Why?"

"Maybe for her protection," Russo said.

"Why? What's happened." Linda asked.

"There have been four murders in Kensington tonight," Russo continued. "All members of a rival mob family of the Antenucci's." He then looked intently into Linda's eyes. "You were aware of Ms. Antenucci's family connections?"

"I've known Angie for many years and know who her relatives are," Linda answered. "She's never been involved with them."

Russo took out a card from his pocket. "Well, if you see Ms. Antenucci have her call me. We'll need to talk," he said as he handed the card to Linda. Within seconds both men had left.

Linda felt goosebumps along her whole body. "Creepy!" she said to herself.

No sooner had she gotten comfortable on the couch when the doorbell rang again.

The impatient visitor rang the doorbell again and again.

"Now what?" Linda mumbled as she rose once again to answer the unwanted visitor.

Rather than look to see who was there or to even ask through the door, Linda swung the door wide open to find a pair of sleazy looking characters waiting with a surprised look on their faces.

"Angela Antenucci?" one of the men asked anxiously.

"No," Linda snapped back. She never got another word out to clarify.

The man pulled a gun and sent a bullet into Linda's chest. In an instant Linda found herself on the floor with blood spilling out onto her white terry robe.

Linda heard the door slam closed as she struggled on the floor in pain, attempting to turn over and get to a telephone to call for help. She realized she had little chance to make it there before bleeding to death.

* * * *

It had been a typical weekday evening for Angela and Benny. She completed her double shift at midnight and Benny was diligently waiting right outside the hospital for her. They had then gone to the all-night dinner, had a light meal and coffee and were now on their way back to Angie's place.

"I'm exhausted!" Angela proclaimed as she slumped in the passenger seat of Benny's car after their meal.

"I'm not surprised," Benny answered her. "Sixteen straight is tough."

Within minutes they were back at her apartment.

"I am so looking forward to going to bed," Angela said at the door.

"So am I," Benny replied with a sly smile on his face.

"I'm sorry, Mister," Angela smiled back at him. "But I hope you understand how tired I really am."

"Just lying next to you is enough for me," Benny said as he hugged Angela by the waist and drew her nearer. "We don't have to have sex every night to be close. Just cuddling next to you is reward enough sometimes."

Angela kissed him softly. "Aren't you sweet."

They kissed again, this time for longer and with more emotion.

"Hey! The door's unlocked," Angie said as she twisted the doorknob.

She swung the door open slowly.

"What's going on?" she said as she cautiously stepped into the apartment.

"Blood!" Benny spoke quietly as he saw a stream of blood extending from the doorway down the hall to the living room and bedrooms.

"Linda!" Angie cried as she clutched Benny's hand and pulled him into the hallway. "Linda! What's going on?"

They followed the blood back toward the bedrooms and found Linda's bloody body face down on the floor at the entrance to her room.

"Is she???" Angie questioned, her voice trembling.

Benny knelt down next to the girl and felt for a pulse. He nodded.

"They were coming after me!" Angie cried as tears began to roll down her cheeks. "They were coming after me."

Benny gently coaxed her away from the body and back down the hallway to the door. "Let's get out of here," he whispered to Angela. "It's not safe!"

* * * *

Benny awoke in the middle of the night in a cold sweat. For a brief time, his nightmare world had brought him back to Vietnam, specifically to the street in Saigon near the embassy and to the explosion.

He awoke with the chills, his body covered with goosebumps and sweat from his head to his toes. His hands were shaking as he reached into his night table and searched for a cigarette to help him once again grasp reality.

As he relived the incident began to change in his mind and the last of these changes troubled Benny.

The same team was there at the beginning. He saw himself, along with Manning, Macon and Ianelli as they walked up the street away from the US Embassy just as always. He saw the truck rounding the corner and the screech of the tires as it speeds up and heads their way. He heard the shouts and cries from the injured and dying as the truck exploded.

Benny saw himself running over to Manning and Macon. His eyes were fixed on Manning as she knelt over Macon's body.

As Benny reached her, he knelt as well and helped her turn over the body.

Instead of Macon's face he saw Angela's surrounded by a strange smoldering body. Her face was tortured by the pain of her wounds, and he could see she was dying. He heard her whisper his name through the pain before awakening from the nightmare.

Benny drew heavily on the smoke. He looked down at the serene face of Angela sleeping beside him. He put out the butt and lay down beside her, caressing her body and feeling her warmth.

His nightmare receded into the back of his mind and became less of a warning as he fell back to sleep again.

* * * *

After a long and agonizing day and night hiding out in Benny's parent's house, Angela finally got up the nerve to contact her family.

She arranged to meet her brother Michael at a restaurant in Center City Philadelphia. When she spoke to him on the phone, Michael seemed very confident that they would be okay to meet out in the open at the popular bistro.

Benny had tried to talk her out of going to meet Michael, remembering what had happened at their last meeting at the diner. He also reminded her of the growing blood bath between the two crime organizations, her family's and the K&A boys, which now had a double-digit body count and occupied the lead story on Action News.

She went anyway.

Even before she entered the restaurant, she could see her brother relaxing at a table by the window puffing away on a cigarette. He didn't pick her up until she had entered the place and was nearing his table.

He did not get up as his sister approached and she sat herself across from him in the booth.

"Any trouble getting here?" Michael asked.

She shook her head nervously. Her throat as so dry she couldn't speak.

"Hey, Angie!" Michael continued. "You've got to get over this. Your girlfriend wasn't the first innocent bystander to get caught up in our mess."

"Linda was my roommate, Michael," Angie strained to get out the words. "They were obviously looking for me when they got to her. More than that she was my friend since Junior High. She didn't deserve to die like that."

"It's water over the dam now," he answered. "Nothing we can do about it except to move on and make sure we get the better of them."

"Except I'm not a part of the organization," Angie countered. "I'm just an innocent bystander, just like Linda was."

"You are part of the family and the organization, Ange," Michael stated. "Whether you like it or not, you are part of this and will be caught up in this mess whether you want to be or not."

"But I'm not like you, Michael," Angela went on with tears in her eyes. "I'm not hard. I'm not tough enough. Look! You're out here at a window seat in the middle of the day just like it's nothing. I'm so afraid I just want to go and hide."

"We can't hide from it, Angie," Michael told her. "We just have to insure that we cover every eventuality when we have to go out in public. Don't you think I checked this place out before I set up this meeting. Don't you think I've got every door covered and have a man at every street corner."

"Do you really trust your instincts that much?" Angie asked back. "Do you really trust your people?"

"Sure do!" Michel answered. He then gestured to one of his men near an exit door to the restaurant. "Hey, Freddie! Come over hear."

The man slowly walked their way.

"Freddie here has known me since High School," Michael went on. "He's been with me his whole life. I trust him like a brother. You'd never do anything to hurt me, would you Freddie?"

"I wouldn't say that" Freddie slowly stated as his face turned up into a wide grin. He raised the pistol he was holding, stared at it a second, pointed it at Michael's chest and fire twice.

"Shit!" Angie screamed as she watched her brother's chest explode as blood and bone splattered up and onto her.

She sprang from the booth, turned, and started to run.

She saw another of Michael's bodyguards start toward her from the other exit with his firearm out and up, pointed at her.

He fired as she turned away toward the back of the restaurant. She felt one shot whiz by her ears followed by a second burst from Freddie's gun that whistled past.

The third shot did not miss its mark. It slammed into her side with a searing pain that caused Angie to let out a scream as she collapsed to the floor.

Immediately afterwards there came the sound of shots being fired from outside the restaurant accompanied by shattering glass which fell on and around Angie as she lay on the floor holding one hand against the bullet hole now oozing blood onto the black and white tiled floor.

As she began to pass out Angie thought about her parents. She didn't know if her brother was alive or dead but suspected the worst and was hoping against hope that her folks wouldn't have to deal with the deaths of both of their children in the same dreadful moment.

* * * *

It took five days for Benny to get access to Jefferson Hospital where they had taken Angela. Each morning he would dutifully show up at Jefferson's main desk and asked to see Angie but was turned away by the hospital personnel.

Each day, when he asked to see her Benny was told she was not being allowed visitors. When he asked about her condition, he was told he was not entitled to that information as he was not a family member.

By the fifth day he was ready to get a lawyer when he was told to take a seat in the waiting area. At least now he hoped he would be getting some answers.

A large man in a plain black suit stood before Benny a few minutes later.

"I'm Detective Jeff Russo," the man began as he flashed a badge in Benny's face. The middle-aged balding man towered over Benny as he sat in one of the many chairs in the waiting area. The expression on his face was stoic and unchanging as he spoke in a monotone.

"How can I help you, Detective?" Benny asked immediately.

"I understand that you are here to see Angela Antenucci," Russo started. "Exactly who are you and what do you have to do with her?"

"My name is Benjamin Lefkowitz," Benny answered quickly. "Angela is a friend of mine."

"You're not a reporter?" the policeman asked.

"No!"

"You're not an attorney?"

"No!"

"Are you a member of the Antenucci family?"

"No!" Benny smiled. "Certainly not with a name like Lefkowitz."

"Are you associated with the K&A gang?"

"Nope!"

"You are from their neighborhood," Russo stated, giving away that he probably knew all the answers before he asked the questions. "How close a friend, then?" he continued.

"Not really your business," Benny answered.

"That tells me you're pretty close," Russo smiled. "Why are you sticking out your neck to see her now?"

Benny looked down at the floor. "She's my girl. I think I love her. I'd like her to know I care."

"Okay, Lefty," the cop concluded. "Let's go up."

"I don't need a police escort."

Russo smiled. "If you're going to see Antenucci you will. She's under heavy police protective custody." He began to walk toward the elevators and Benny followed.

"Is that necessary?" Benny asked as he and Russo stepped into the elevator.

Russo shot him a curious look. "Yes!"

The elevator stopped at the 6th floor and both men got out. They passed two uniformed officers on their way to room 614.

"I'll give you a few moments with her," Russo said as he stopped at the door allowing Benny to enter the room.

Angela was lying in bed connected to a number of monitors, each beeping in time to her heartbeat. She looked pale and drawn, but not in pain. When she saw Benny at the foot of the bed she smiled slightly, and her dimples immediately appeared and lit up the room.

"Benny," she whispered in a strained, hoarse voice. She raised her arm up slightly and he reached out and took her hand. "I'm so happy to see you."

"How are you doing?" he asked. He felt himself choking up.

"No worse for wear," she continued to smile, but he could tell she was forcing it. "It's been a tough few days."

"You'll be fine," he reassured her.

"I know," she answered. "That's what the doctors have to say. Just hope the cops let me go when the time comes."

"Right now you just rest," Benny went on. "When the doctors say you're good to go I'm sure the police won't hold you here. You've done nothing wrong."

Angie cringed as a jolt of pain seemed to run through her body. "Don't bet on it. They've got me now and won't let me go. I'm a bargaining chip to my family."

"I'm sure it will be okay. The cops are here to protect you from the K&A gang. They just want to make sure you stay safe."

She shook her head. "I don't believe that for a moment. When I'm able to go they'll find a way to keep an eye on me."

Benny squeezed her hand. "Don't worry about that now. Just get better so I can take you home."

She cringed again as she tried to move. "Listen to me! I don't want you coming back here. You need to stay as far away from me as you can. Get out of here now and don't come back!"

Benny leaned in and kissed her. He could see the tears in her eyes as he caressed her. "I will be back. I'll be here for you."

* * * *

Angela knew she was feeling better as she awoke on her sixth day in the hospital. As she looked at herself in the small mirror imbedded in the hospital table, she could see the color coming back to her face. Also, the dark lines that surrounded her eyes were nearly gone. Now, if only the doctors would tell her when she would be leaving.

She also wondered exactly how and where she would be going once she left Jefferson Hospital. She still had a police guard at her door, but she had been told by Detective Russo that the cops were there for her protection. She knew she had done nothing wrong. She knew that she just happened to be at the wrong place and at the wrong time when she was caught in the crossfire at her brother's assassination.

As she laid in her hospital bed, she still had doubts as to whether the cops would let her just walk out of the hospital. She worried that she was actually a target of the K&A gang. She received no other visitors except for Benny, who had been allowed to visit her briefly for the last two days. She certainly did not expect anyone from her family to visit her with all the police around.

Yet, as the afternoon began, she saw her father get off the nearby elevator and walk slowly with the assistance of his walker to her room. Surprisingly, he was alone.

"Pop," Angie immediately questioned him as he entered her room. "What are you doing here?"

"What?" Sal Antenucci asked back in his gruff South Philly voice. "Why shouldn't I visit my daughter lying in a hospital bed. What kind of father would I be if I didn't come?"

"I know but aren't you putting yourself at risk by coming here?" she asked back. "Aren't you a target?"

"Not so much," he said as he flopped down into the chair next to her bed. "I'm just an old man. Not so much a power in our family business as you might expect. The power is in other people's hands for now……not our family's.

Angie felt herself beginning to sob as tears welled up inside her. "I'm so sorry for what happened to Michael," she choaked out the words. "It was my fault. I should have never insisted on seeing him that day."

"It's not your fault, Angie," her father told her. "Michael was a hothead who made a lot of enemies and placed his faith in some people who weren't trustworthy. He was betrayed and you just got caught in the crossfire."

"If I didn't ask to see him he wouldn't have been exposed like that."

"He would have found another way to fuck up," Sal Antenucci waved his hands as he spoke. "The kid was like a loose cannon. Sooner or later, he would be caught with his pants down. Don't get me wrong, I loved your brother as much as any man could love a son, but I knew his shortcomings and just chose to ignore them. So, his death was my fault more than it was yours, Angie! I should have kept him hidden."

"Sorry, Pop."

"Aw, don't sweat it," Sal snapped back. "I'm an old bird. I'll get over it pretty quick. I'm more concerned about you, kid. I'm worried the boys from K&A will go after you."

"I'm kinda worried about that too," Angela admitted.

"Here's what you have to do," Sal continued. "When they let you go from here you've got to come home to Christian Street. We'll keep you safe until this mess is over. You can't go back to Kensington. Am I clear?"

"Perfectly," Angie answered. At this point she wasn't going to argue the point.

"And," her father went on. "You've got to dump this Jew boyfriend of yours, what's his name....Benny something! I don't trust him."

"Benny's been the only one standing by me through all this," Angie answered. "I can't dump him now. I think we're in love."

"Love is overrated," Sal retorted. "Family is what matters. Come back to the family, Angela, for your own safety."

He slowly rose up from the chair, held his daughter's hand and kissed her on her forehead. As he walked out of her room he repeated. "Come back to the family, Angela."

* * * *

It was going to be a good day for Benny. He had been told by the nurses that Angela would be released today. He had come prepared to take her home. He was not going to take her back to her apartment in Kensington, nor to his parent's place in the neighborhood. Benny had rented a new apartment in the Northeast for them and had taken some of her clothes from her place as well as his clothes and furniture he had just bought at Levitz.

He felt himself bouncing as he walked through the hospital. He was happy that he wouldn't have to come back here again. He was happy that Angela had sufficiently recovered from her wounds to allow her to leave and, hopefully, allow them to resume their life together without the shadow of her family and the gang war that still enveloped the city.

As he neared her room after getting off the elevator, he noticed that the Police guard was no longer there and that her room was empty and already cleaned and prepped for the next patient.

"Where's Angela Antenucci?" he asked the nurse at the station across from Angela's room.

"She's discharged," the woman answered. "Left earlier this morning. She took her entourage of cops with her ….thankfully!"

"Shit," Benny mumbled to himself. He wondered where the police had taken her to and knew she hadn't done anything to be arrested.

"You Benny Lefkowitz?" the nurse asked.

Benny meekly nodded.

"She left this for you," the nurse said as she handed him an envelope with his name scrawled across it. He recognized Angie's handwriting.

He waited for the isolation of the family waiting room before he opened the envelope. He silently, slowly read it to himself.

"Dear Benny: Sorry you have to find out this way, but you already know that I have left the hospital without you. I have gone back home to my family. There I am protected. Staying with you would have exposed both of us to too much danger. It's better this way. Forget about me. Get on with your life. Please remember that I love you and what we had together, but this is for the best. Love, Angela."

Benny read the letter twice before folding it back into the envelope and placing it in his pocket. He then quietly left the hospital.

* * * *

As the days past Benny had a tough time getting Angela out of his mind. Her face haunted his dreams and his thoughts of her, and what might have been, haunted his daydreams. He thought about, and quickly dismissed any efforts to get in contact with her. The Antenucci's had her locked away in their South Philly stronghold and Benny knew he couldn't penetrate their lair to get to her.

The evening news each night was splattered with the continuing conflict between the two rival mobs. One night the K&A boys would hit a South Philly joint. The next night Antenucci's gang would retaliate. And the cycle continued every few days and the body count rose.

Benny, somewhat depressed because he knew too much about the gang war and the woman he still loved, sat down in his recliner to watch the eleven o'clock news.

He clicked on his TV and watched as the glow came on and lit up his darkened living room. He had tuned in just in time as the Action News theme resounded from the set.

"And the big story tonight is another escalation in the mob warfare that has gripped the city," the commentor said at the end of headlines. "However, this time, it might signal an end to the violence as key players are among the victims."

The newscaster droned on. "There were four shootings tonight. Two in South Philadelphia and two in Kensington and two people are dead. One of the victims is Frank Kelly, the longtime second in command within the K&A organization."

A picture flashed onscreen of a middle-aged balding man who looked more a bookkeeper than a crime boss.

"The second victim was found in an alley in South Philadelphia near Second and Snyder. Her name was Angela Antenucci, the daughter of crime boss Salvatore Antenucci."

An old picture of Angela's popped up on the screen. Benny remembered it as her high school graduation picture. Her hair was longer, but she still had that full, haunting smile on her face and her dimples accentuated her beauty.

Benny stared at her beautiful face until the picture faded and another story began.

Benny shut off the television set and sat in the darkness. Angela's image seemed to dwell in Benny's eyes as the quiet night continued.

Short Time

The late edition of the Daily News had just arrived. Frank Kozicki took out the cutters he kept under the counter and quickly snapped the band that held the bundle of newspapers together. The bundle seemed to breathe as the band broke, as if the papers had a life of their own.

Fire in South Philly was the headline this afternoon. The words, written in bold broad letters across the top of the paper, seemed to jump out at him. *November 14th, 1984* was the date at the top of the paper. *Cool and Cloudy, Winds Increasing,* read the weather at the other end of the banner page.

As he stared at the street scene from the front of his newsstand, the brisk, cold fall wind seemed to swirl around him. The men and women, hurrying home from work, were bundled against the chill. Frank could feel the cold through his warm woolen coat. He could hear the whistle of the wind in his ears as it drowned out the sounds of the neighborhood.

Suddenly the whine of a police siren invaded the air and took the place of the whistle of the wind. A second later the police car came into view as it roared around the corner onto Allegheny Avenue from Kensington. The back wheels squealed as it raced to complete the turn and swerved to avoid the steel pole that supported the elevated train tracks.

Frank watched as another car screamed past him and both of them came to halt just up the street.

The police scurried from their cars and others seemed to come out of nowhere, their guns drawn, and their eyes fixed on the front of the office building in the middle of the block.

It was sundown, and on this fall evening the streetlights were just beginning to glisten, the lights from the just hung Christmas decorations suspended from the elevated train supports sparkled to life, but the rhythmic pulse of the police car's lights dominated the street and kept the eyes of every bystander fixed on the frantic spectacle unfolding in the street.

"Come on!" the deep voice of sergeant Mike Rossi boomed to the crowd that stood by Frank's news stand. "Move along, folks! There's nothing to see."

A series of gun shots echoed through the air!

The pigeons nestled in the crevasses below the El tracks scattered in a flurry of wings and feathers. People scattered too, as a mild panic took hold on the street.

Frank stood by this news stand, seemingly without fear, but his heart pounded loudly in his chest as he crooked his neck to see up the street.

"Jeez!" Sergeant Mike gulped. "What the hell!"

The crackle of gunshots again!

"Someone's been shot!" Frank heard from up Allegheny Avenue.

"Call an ambulance!"

Dillon and Domishevski, two beat cops Frank knew well, came running toward him from the scene of the shooting. Between them, wrapped in their arms, was a small man. Frank recognized him as Marty Kline, a plainclothes detective from the local precinct. The man looked white as a sheet.

"You got some water in there, Frank? Or some towels?" Dillon panted, his breath forming clouds in the cold air. He and the other officer had laid the detective on the ground in front of Frank's newsstand.

Frank Kozicki stared at the man, saw the blood covering his chest, watched a pillar of red squirt into the air, and was frozen.

"Frank!" Dillon repeated. "Did you hear me?"

Still Frank didn't move.

Another plainclothesman suddenly came into view. It was Jake Pageant, Kline's partner. Frank knew them both well. He had offered them both coffee on many a cold morning here at K&A.

"Did someone call it in?" Pageant asked, his voice choked with dread as he looked at his partner. "Does anyone know a doctor nearby?"

No one answered. No one moved.

Pageant knelt next to Kline as another small fountain of blood shot skyward. "Damned, this looks bad," he whispered. "Marty. Marty! Hang on, short timer! Hang on!"

Rossi ran up and knelt next to Pageant and the dying cop. "Ambulance is on its way. Just keep him still.......and, Jake.......they got him."

"Too late."

Frank watched the body of Marty Kline shudder and then become still.

"Damn!" Pageant said. "Only six weeks, Marty! Only six weeks!"

* * * *

They found the first body three months later, Frank Kozicki would remember. They found him near the back door to Kelly's Korner up near York and Dauphin. Frank remembered the grizzly headlines as the newspapers that passed his newsstand reported the news and the developments in the case every day for a week.

The police were close to solving the murder of the homeless old man. He was only a dead wino, but his murder and the way the Daily News played it up had captured the people's imagination. It was just another example of how crime seemed to have gripped the city.

The police were close, the papers said, but Frank Kozicki knew better, Jake Pageant and his new partner were on the job. Jake had talked to Frank every day as they shared coffee on the cold winter mornings. Jake confessed that he had no answers, he didn't know who committed the murder of the derelict. Jake confessed that he could search for an answer until the day he retired and never find it.

Eventually the stories in the papers died down. First, they were replaced on the front pages by newer news. Later, items on the police investigation vanished from the middle of the paper as well. Finally, Jake confessed to the newsstand owner, the police put the investigation on the back burner for good.

That was two days before the second body was found.

* * * *

There was something about the locker room at the precinct house. It was something Mike Rossi remembered distinctly, an atmosphere of mildew and sweat and soap. It had a mustiness that seemed to overshadow the cold draft that blew through the place from the open windows that lined the top of the wall. Mike could hear the faint sounds of traffic on Front Street that came through the windows. He could hear it clearly, even though the room was filled with men talking, laughing, and arguing.

Mike just wanted to quietly drift into the room. He wanted to find his locker, deposit his belongings, and disappear without being noticed. He didn't want to bear the brunt of jokes about being the rookie detective in the precinct. He didn't want to be singled out by these veterans as a cop who moved up so quickly from walking a beat.

Mike just didn't want to be noticed in his father's old precinct. Not yet anyway.

He knew he was asking the impossible.

"Ah," he heard the familiar voice of Stash Domishevski as he tiptoed behind the heavyset old patrolman. "Dem Iggles. Dey ain't got nothin'. Three weeks into the season and you can take 'em out of the oven. They're done."

"Shut up, Stash," Joey Dillon, another one of Mike's pop's friends answered. "Give 'em a break. They played some pretty good teams so far."

Joey's eyes met Mike and the young detective quickly turned his head away. He quickly and quietly moved to the corner locker with his name newly stenciled in. *M Rossi, Jr.* stood out clear and bold in white paint against the old gray locker. They may as well have installed a neon sign.

"Well, well, well," Joey's voice echoed into Mike's ears as the tall, thin old man came up from behind. "If it ain't little Mikey, the boy wonder."

Mike inhaled deeply and turned to face Joey. "How ya doin', Mr. Dillon? Mr. Domishevski?"

The hulking figure of Stash Domishevski stood behind Dillon as they both sneered at the new detective. They looked remarkably like Laurel and Hardy. Mike wanted to laugh, but successfully struggled to hold it in.

"We're doing fine," Stash answered. "Hey kid! You nervous?" The man had a large grin on his face, but his eyes seemed to sparkle with genuine concern.

Mike had known both men all his life and was a little embarrassed. Most five-year patrolmen didn't make detective on their first try at the exam. He had been lucky, if drawing an assignment in his father's old precinct in his old neighborhood could be considered luck. He'd now have to work side by side with officers who remembered him when he was in diapers. They were men he respected and now he could be placed into the position of giving them orders.

"Yeah, I'm nervous," he smiled as he turned his face away from the men. "You guys know more about me than anyone but my folks."

"Maybe more," Joey said. "But don't you worry, kid. We're not here to put you down. Anything you want, any help you need, you just ask."

Mike Rossi felt his heartbeat slow again to a normal pace. He felt better when he heard the reassuring words from the beat cops. They'd give him every chance to fit in, he knew.

"Who'd they assign you to?" Stash asked.

It was customary for a rookie detective to draw as a partner one of older guys on the floor. Mike guessed that Stash and Joey knew all the detectives here well. He was looking forward toward their opinion. Proudly, he told them. "I'm going to partner with Jake Pageant,"

"Jeez," Stash's face turned sour. "That's too bad."

"How do you mean?"

Joey explained. "Pageant used to be a pretty good detective, but...." his voice trailed off.

"Go on," Mike prodded. "I want to know."

"Well, Jake used to be the best, you know," Stash picked it up. "He was sharp as a knife in picking up them clues. Then, about a year ago, his partner was gunned down in a shootout at K&A. You remember?"

"Yeah, yeah," Mike jumped in. "That big shoot out at the old PECO building. Pop was there. The police commissioner came down here and everything. I remember going to the funeral with Pop."

Joey continued. "Yeah, well that was Pageant's partner and he ain't been the same since. He has worked on one case but hasn't solved it. Those derelict murders, you know. Some of the guys here think he's just riding it out...."

short-timers attitude. But Jake keeps pushing, so that ain't so. It's not like he's acting like a short timer, the captain would see that, but he's just had nothing but bad luck since Marty Kline died. His last partner, he got discouraged and transferred out."

"I guess you'll be next," Stash almost laughed.

"I'm sure it can't be that bad," Mike said.

"Let's hope not, kid," Joey said as he placed his long thin hand on Mike's shoulder. "Working with a short-timer like Jake ain't the best way to start a promising career, but it may be the way to end one."

* * * *

The captain met Mike Rossi, Jr. at the front desk of the precinct. The captain was a new man, Mike knew, who didn't remember his dad. Mike thought this would be an advantage. There'd be no comparisons, no memories for the captain to recollect of Sergeant Mike Rossi, Sr., now retired, or Mikey.

The captain introduced himself and Vollmer, the desk sergeant. Mike didn't tell the captain that he had known Vollmer for years. After a brief and very redundant tour of the precinct, the captain took his new rookie out to meet his partner on the streets of Kensington.

As they rode in the new police car, Mike recognized so many of the sights around him. He watched as people's heads turned as they rode down Westmoreland Street toward the Avenue. He wondered if they recognized him but doubted they did. As they passed by the Ascension Church Mike remembered his days there. He remembered the white shirts and ties he wore since he was six and remembered telling himself how he'd never wear a uniform again. Maybe, he thought to himself, that was what drove him to become a detective. Anything to be out of that uniform.

They parked near K&A and the Captain took Mike to the busy intersection. It was a typical fall afternoon, cool and crisp as the wind blew fallen leaves, scraps of paper and specks of dirt into little twisters that drifted up and down the sidewalk.

"You see Pageant?" the captain asked old man Kozicki as he reached his cluttered news stand.

Kozicki, a weathered old man without any teeth, shook his head.

"Funny, he said he'd meet me here."

"Ain't seen him yet, Sir." Kozicki said. "But if Detective Pageant said he'd meet you here, he'll be here."

"By the way, Frank," the captain went on. "This is......."

Kozicki smiled a broad toothless smile and extended a hand across the stacks of papers. "Mike Rossi!" I'd know you anywhere. How you doin', kid?"

Mike smiled back as he shook the man's hand, permanently stained with newsprint ink. "Nice to see you again, Mr. Kozicki."

"How's your pop?"

"Fine."

"Send my regards, will ya."

Mike nodded.

"Well then," the captain said as he looked at this watch. "Since you two already know each other and since I have another appointment, I'll leave you here, Rossi. I'm sure Pageant will be along shortly."

In a second, the captain was gone.

"Funny duck, ain't he, kid." Kozicki sneered as he watched the captain go. "They just ain't the same, them cops from Chestnut Hill."

"Is that where he's from?"

"Gotta be." Kozicki's toothless grin was from ear to ear. "Sure ain't from here."

"Got any coffee, Frank." Another voice intruded from behind him. Mike quickly turned and saw a small, thin man standing there bundled in an old trench coat and broad brimmed hat. He looked like he was from another age, the fifties rather than the eighties.

"Sure, Jake." Kozicki said. "Hey, Jake, you remember Mike Rossi's kid," he said as he waved at Mike.

"Hey, how are ya." Pageant nodded. There was a familiar look on his face, as if he had seen this man before, which Mike knew he must have, but the patrolmen rarely became friendly with the detectives in the precinct. It was an unspoken class distinction between the beat cops and the suits.

"So, you're Mike Rossi's kid." Pageant said with a snarl. The detective looked like he was in his sixties, with a wrinkled round face, wispy gray hair and a double chin. His blue eyes still sparkled, however, just like they must have when he was a youthful eager young sprout like Mike.

"Yes, sir." Mike smiled and extended his hand. "I'm Mike, Jr."

"You're my new partner, eh, kid?" Pageant grunted. Mike couldn't decide if it was a question or a statement.

"Yes, sir."

"Okay, Junior." Pageant sneered. His voice had an irritating nasal quality. "Get a cup of joe and I'll fill you in. We've got a lot of work to do."

For the next hour, Jake Pageant and Mike walked around the neighborhood while he gave the rookie a detailed picture of the case he'd been involved with for over a year. There had been three murders in the past year, all derelicts beaten to death in spots around the neighborhood. The murders weren't very frequent, Pageant explained, so they weren't after some nut who's out to make a splash, yet every time the investigation seemed to hit a dead end another bum would be found in a dark alley with his brains beaten in. It was just enough to keep him and his partner busy, but not enough to raise the furor of the populous, not since the first week of the first murder, anyway.

"These bums and winos." Jake's voice showed his contempt. "They're overrunning the neighborhood anyway. They got no relatives. They got nobody who cares. No one's getting excited about this guy killing off a few bums."

"How do you know they're all done by the same guy?" Mike asked as he looked over the grizzly pictures Jake pulled from his pocket.

"Cause I do," Jake snapped. "The weapon's the same. The circumstances and most of all, the timing. He knows we're out there looking for him. He knows we're snooping around. He senses when we've given up looking to solve the last one and knocks off another one to keep our interest. He wants our attention."

"If you're so close, why can't you.... well, you know."

Jake smiled. His eyes lit up. "I know what you're thinking, kid. Why can't I solve this one? Well, kid, sometimes it's just the breaks, you know. Sometimes, it's just the breaks."

* * * *

The report came in early in the morning, three days after Mike Rossi, Jr. was hooked up with Jake Pageant.

It had been three days during which Mike read every word of every report in the files on their serial killer case. It had been three frustrating days of listening to Jake mow down every idea that came into Mike's head. It had been three very educational days as Mike learned how much Jake knew about this case and his job in general.

Jake Pageant seldom missed a trick, Mike realized as he read the old detective's reports and as he listened to him remember the facts of each murder. He knew it would be an education just to watch the master in action. Now, he had his chance.

The body was found by two cops patrolling on Somerset Street, just before the night shift ended. The news of the next victim greeted Jake and Mike as they walked in the door. Without even taking the lids off their coffees they headed toward the crime scene.

The place was already cordoned off and surrounded by policemen and specialists from downtown. They were doing their usual work, dusting for fingerprints, taking photos. They barely looked up when Jake and Mike arrived, they nodded at Jake and then resumed their work.

"Who found him?" Jake immediately asked a cluster of uniforms huddled together against the cold.

Two youngish cops, one male and one female, politely raised their hands.

"Michael." Pageant waved at Rossi. "Get their statements while I look around."

Before Mike could utter a sound the senior detective had vanished, leaving him to take the young officers' statements.

Ten minutes later Mike had squeezed everything he could out of the uniforms and searched for his partner. He was nowhere to be found.

They had already placed the body on a stretcher, covered it in plastic and were ready to haul it away. The photographers were putting away their cameras and the coroner and his team were closing up shop. Mike's head was spinning. He couldn't remember a thing. He was just a bystander. He hadn't had a chance to investigate anything.

"You lost, kid?" one of the uniforms asked.

"Where's Pageant?"

"Up the street." The officer pointed. There was a sneer in his voice, as if he was laughing at the young detective.

Mike found Pageant the second he turned the next corner. He was staring off toward Lehigh Avenue.

"He came from up there," Pageant softly said as Mike Rossi joined him. "From up on the train tracks this side of Lehigh."

"How do you know?"

"The victim was drunk," Pageant went on. "The broken bottle of cheap wine didn't leave much of a puddle, so it was near empty. That swill makes the winos warm and sleepy real fast, so the victim wasn't watching too close to who came up behind him, but he knew to watch the street, they all do.

"The killer had to sneak up on him or else he'd have tried to move. The victim was found right next to the steam vent, like he hadn't moved an inch. That means the killer silently came up behind him, clubbed him about five or six times, and vanished back toward the rail yard."

"How about the weapon?" Mike asked.

Pageant shrugged. "Not left, as usual. But the forensic will find it was a smooth barreled club, probably less than two feet long.........like a billy club."

"Should we search up there?" Mike pointed toward the elevated freight yard that paralleled Lehigh Avenue.

"Nope." Pageant looked down and unconsciously kicked a small pebble on the sidewalk. "He's been here for hours. The killer's long gone, and so are the rest of the clues."

* * * *

"This man is uncanny." Mike Rossi knew he sounded like a schoolboy as he spoke, but he admired Jack Pageant. He looked at his beer, smacked his lips and continued. "He knew just what to look for, what to ignore. He knew where to go, how to put it all together."

Gwen Smith looked back at him from across the restaurant's small table. She had a bored, sleepy-eyed look on her face. Her huge round eyes were half closed.

Gwen loved Mike Rossi but couldn't stand when he wanted to talk shop. She never cared about police work, especially the boring details. At least when Joe Friday worked on a case it was over in thirty minutes. Mike could take longer than that to explain a coffee break.

"Gwen?" Mike finally caught on. "Are you listening to me?"

She blinked and her long, thin, elegant face turned up into a sweet smile. "Oh, sure, Michael. Your partner's a genius."

"He's a very good, very solid investigator," Mike snapped back. "A total pro."

"Then why hasn't he solved this wino killer thing? It's been over a year."

Mike couldn't answer that, and the conversation crept into silence.

Gwen stared back at Mike as the young detective struggled to find an answer. Sometimes, she realized, he acted just like a child. He was quick to make up his mind, many times without thinking, and quick to show admiration, or envy, at another's accomplishments. She feared he was doing this with his new detective partner, whom he had already admitted couldn't solve this case that he seemed to know everything about.

"Just how good can Jake Pageant be if he can't solve this crime?" she almost whined, praying that her protestations would cause Mike to drop the subject of work. "I mean, four murders, a whole year and you guys are no nearer."

He sighed. "I know, but it can't be Jake's fault."

He was ready to go on, but she interrupted him before the words could emerge from his gaping mouth. "Can we drop this? I don't want to spend the whole night on police business. I don't expect you to take an interest in my schoolwork, now do I?"

"Your schoolwork is boring," Mike countered.

She smiled. "Not half as boring as your work seems to me."

"Wait a minute!" Mike said. Gwen could almost visualize the light bulb going off inside Mike's brain. "Have you found a subject for your final thesis yet?"

Her brain told her to be wary of his thoughts, but she honestly answered. "No."

Gwen was in her final year at Temple University. To her, the college was like a big high school except that she met Mike there, someone she'd have never met otherwise. Gwen wasn't from Kensington. She grew up in the Northeast and commuted to college every day, naturally by the El that passed by K&A. It seemed that almost daily she saw this handsome guy get on at 5th Street and get off at Allegheny. They'd look at each other, first staring, then smiling, but never talking. Then one day she saw him on the quad at Temple and he finally approached her. Little did she know what she was in for. Never did she expect to be so involved with a guy, a cop no less, from K&A.

Mike and she had little in common on the surface. They grew up in drastically different neighborhoods, were from different cultures and took different paths in life. Yet there was something that joined them together, although neither of them could seem to say what it was in words. They knew it only when they looked in each other's eyes, when they smiled and when they kissed. They knew there was something inside that drew them together, each day more than the last.

"What's up your sleeve?" Gwen asked Mike as she thought about her thesis. She was a journalism major, and she had to do one detailed piece on the daily life of a person before getting her degree.

"Wouldn't Jake make a great subject?"

She twisted her face into a sour expression. "I don't know...."

Mike reached across his table and took her hand. Gwen felt the warmth from inside him rushing up her arm. "Come on Gwen. At least think about it."

"Okay," she heard her mouth say the words, but her brain silently was protesting. "I'll think about it."

* * * *

Gwen noticed the sparkle in the man's eyes from the moment she met him. It was just like a wink, accompanied by a sneer that crossed his face. He reminded her of Popeye, except that the pipe was missing. He was actually leering at her and she felt embarrassed and knew she was blushing. Her eyes had to turn away from him, even though she knew he wasn't looking at her face anymore. He had seen her eyes and her pretty smile. Now he concentrated on the rest of her.

"So, you're Mikey's little girl-friend," Jake Pageant sneered as he finished surveying her from head to toe. He obviously liked what he saw.

"Yes, Detective Pageant," she answered. Her voice sounded unusually squeaky to her own ears. She had goose bumps and her hand quivered as she extended it to him. "Michael has told me so much about you."

"He has, has he," Pageant continued to sneer as he gently shook Gwen's hand. His palm was cold and clammy and its touch extended a chill up her arm. The signals from her body told her that she didn't like this man. "Hope it's all been big fat lies," he continued.

"What do you mean?"

"Well, if he told you the truth, I'd be just some old fart that he's stuck with for a partner." Jake almost laughed. "I'd like it better if you'd see me as Dick Tracy."

Gwen unconsciously smiled. "Oh, it's more Dick Tracy, Detective Pageant."

"Jake. Call me Jake."

"Okay, Jake. Did Michael tell you why I wanted to talk to you?"

Jake's smile vanished. "Nope, and where is that guy of yours anyway?"

She gestured back toward the rear of the lobby. "He just went back there for a minute. I don't know whether he's calling in or what."

"Ah! He probably just had to make a pit stop."

"Well, anyway." Gwen continued. "He asked me to talk to you."

Jake took hold of her elbow and pulled her over to a bench in the corner of the bank lobby. As they walked, their footsteps echoed on the marble floor of the cavernous old bank. The sounds seemed to resound off the high ceiling and hit her ears louder than it was before. She wondered if it was a good idea to talk to him in the bank. If the sounds of their voices echoed in the same way, everyone was going to hear.

"So, what's up?" Jake asked.

"Well, Detect......I mean, Jake," Gwen began after taking a nervous deep breath. "I'm a senior journalism major at Temple and Michael, he knows I have an important paper to submit chronicling the daily life of someone. Michael, suggested that you'd be a great subject, sort of a modern-day Sherlock Holmes or something. He admires you, you know, Mike does. He thinks you're something special." Gwen ended with a wide smile on her face.

Jake didn't smile back. He just sniffed. "Listen, little lady. I don't want to be nobody's term paper, you know. Jeez, I ain't nothing special. I'm just an old cop winding down the last days of his working life. I get up each morning, put on my pants the same way as anybody. I go off to work and go home at the end of each day. Just that I'm a cop instead of.... say, a banker. I'm no Sherlock Holmes, just a tired old man."

"You're not that old."

"Listen, girl!" Jake shot back. "I'm fifty-four years old. I'm going to be fifty-five in three months, and I can retire. Dammit! I can't wait. I've been working around this neighborhood for some thirty-five years. I've seen it changed a lot in that time, gettin' old just like me. I've rescued cats from trees. I've investigated missing dogs and kids. I've shooed bums off people's stoops and, yeah, I've seen murders and dead bodies and drug addicts up at McPherson Square with needles sticking out of them. I'm old and tired and not half as noble as the kind of guy you're looking for in your story."

"Maybe you are, Jake," Gwen insisted. "Maybe Sherlock Holmes wasn't a good analogy. I think you'd make a great subject. An ordinary man in his last days before retiring."

Jake snorted. "Yeah, well, I don't think so. Look, Miss Smith, I'm not going to beat around the bush. I'm just hanging in there, waiting for retirement. I've got a little place up in the Poconos, right on a lake. In three months,

I'm going to kiss this place good-bye and head up there. I don't want to know what's going down in this dump after I leave. I just want to fish, eat and drink beer. I got no wife, no kids, and few friends. I'm dull as an old kitchen knife, and I'm not interested in your story."

"But, Jake...." Gwen tried to interrupt.

He wouldn't let her. "And I don't want no bleeding-heart little chippy following me around right now," he snapped. "You got it."

The man stared at her with anger. She knew when to shut up.

"You don't think I'm a nice guy," Jake sneered. "Well, like Durocher said, they finish last. My old partner, Marty, he was a nice guy. He was six weeks from hangin' them up when, bam, they plugged a hole in him right on the corner outside this bank. He was a nice guy, but he didn't get to see his retirement. I'm going to see mine, you got it girl, and I don't need you trailing after me right now."

"I'm sorry." Gwen couldn't even look at him.

"Well." Mike had returned, a wide self-satisfied grin on his face. "You two get acquainted?"

"Yeah, Mike." Jack glared up at him. "And you can take you little girl-friend home now. I think she's had enough."

Mike looked at Gwen's red face and knew. "I take it things didn't go so well?"

Without replying, Gwen got up from the bench and fled the bank, her footsteps echoing loudly in her ears.

"Things went fine for me," Jake answered with a big smile.

* * * *

It had been another long, hard day for Frank Kozicki. As he got older Frank realized that the winters were getting harder and harder to get through. It was one thing standing all day, something Frank had done all his life. It was another to withstand the aching cold that even his little space heater couldn't overcome. And the dampness, that seemed to bother him the most as the years passed. It seemed to get into his bones, the cold and the dampness, and he couldn't shake it out, couldn't warm up. Not even a warm bath seemed to help. Only the booze seemed to take away the painful, cold ache.

Used to be that Frank would keep his stand open later than he did now. Used to be that he would keep it open on weekends, even Saturday nights, when he'd do a fortune in Sunday Inquirers. Now he opened only Monday through Friday, rush hour to rush hour, and his profits were down a lot. That was one blessing about the state of the neighborhood and his own getting old. He couldn't have taken the long hours, especially this winter, but it wasn't safe to be open at night anymore.

Kensington sure had changed, Frank Kozicki realized as he set the alarm on the stand and bolted the padlocked door. Used to be he didn't worry about having an alarm. Used to be that his stand didn't get broken into every month or so. Used to be he kept some money in there every night. Not anymore.

Used to be that Kensington was a nice place to live and the Avenue was safe. Basically, the neighborhood still was okay, at least some parts, but not the Avenue. Not at night. Now the air smelled of cheap whiskey and there were needles hidden in every corner. Frank even found them around his news stand sometimes.

Used to be that the Avenue was alive even two weeks after Christmas. Used to be the place to shop. Now, instead of families looking in store windows after dark, it was bands of toughs on the streets and bums shivering next to the steel gates that hung over every store front. The families, even the ones from Kensington and Fishtown, they were up on Aramingo Avenue shopping, or in the suburban malls.

Used to be one felt safe on the street after dark, Frank remembered. Now he felt only as safe as the gun he kept in his pocket let him feel. Now he felt safe only with it clutched in his fingers.

As he drifted toward home, up quiet Allegheny Avenue, Frank remembered the Automat and the Midway movie theater, the stores and the homes that lined the busy street. The Automat was gone, so was the movie theater. The stores, for the most part, were gone and many of the homes were boarded up as well. He knew that on the small side streets life went on much the same as it did when he first moved to Kensington forty years ago, but the Avenue was dead. K&A was dead.

Frank would be glad to leave. He looked forward to closing up the news stand for the last time. He looked forward to warm summer nights, fishing by the pond. He looked forward to cool fall days, watching the tube with a beer in his hand and a dog at his feet. Next year. Next spring. He reminded himself as his body shivered against a cold gust of wind, one last winter before he'd call it quits.

"Hey!" Frank heard a raspy voice call to him. "Yo! You got something for me?"

He looked over at two familiar bums that always seemed to be resting on the steam vent on this corner. They were dirty and unshaven, dressed in layers of old coats. Frank couldn't guess how old they were, but they looked younger than him. Just down on their luck, they had told him, but he had little sympathy for them.

Frank Kozicki took the pint bottle out of his pocket. He took one last swig of the Tennessee whiskey and felt an instant jolt of warmth from his head to his toes. He screwed the top on tight and looked at the ounce or two that was left in the bottle.

"Here you go," he said as he tossed the bottle toward the bums.

"Thanks, Mister."

"Yeah. Get a job."

* * * *

"I'm frustrated," Mike said. Though his voice sounded angry, the sour look from Gwen made him realize that he was whining like a little boy. "I've just about had it. Now I know why Jake's other partners quit.

"Then why don't you?" Gwen purred. She couldn't help it as she smiled with a cat-like quality, a self-satisfied sneer. "I just knew you'd have no patience."

He shook his head. "Patience is one thing, Gwen, but it really hurts to realize that after five months I'm no closer than when I started."

"How does Jake feel about this?" she asked as she poured coffee from Mike's ancient coffee pot into a pair of large ceramic mugs.

Michael Rossi. Jr. began to pace his small apartment. He was silent as Gwen watched him move in a slow circle, touching the relics of his life as he went. He picked up a baseball he said he caught at the Vet. Mike Schmidt's name was on it, supposedly from a shot to left, but Gwen new better. It was store bought.

He passed the pictures of his folks and his big brother that rested on a small table behind the sofa. Gwen bet Mike couldn't look his dad in the face right now. The old policeman would have dressed him down if he talked about quitting.

He leaned against the mantel of the fake fireplace and stared at his commendation, a small wooden plaque they gave him for valor during some incident in his old precinct in West Philly. Mike probably feels he'd have to return that if he gave up on Jake Pageant and the un-solved serial murder, Gwen thought.

She felt sorry for him as he struggled to put the pieces of the case back together. She decided her man needed her help.

Again, she repeated. "How does Jake feel?"

Mike closed his eyes. "He hasn't changed. He still thinks he's close."

"Look, Michael, maybe if we went over it, you and me. Maybe I can help you put your finger on something both of you have overlooked."

"I can't really discuss the case with you," he said. "You know that."

She laughed. "Oh, that's a good one. You lived this case, you know. It's been part of your life, maybe a bigger part than me, for the whole winter. Don't you think that the married detectives discuss their cases with their wives?"

"But we're not married."

"That's right, but that's never stopped you in the past."

He shook his head. "That was different. This is a murder case."

"Murder. Robbery." Gwen got up from the sofa and leaned on him. "What's the difference, Michael? Maybe I can help." She planted a small, but wet kiss on his cheek.

He took a deep breath. "Okay."

"Okay. Then tell me what you know."

Mike outlined most of the facts for her, never looking her in the eyes as he rambled on. Most of the time he stared at the ceiling as he reviewed the evidence. The cause of death in all five cases was the same, blows to the head. The coroner's assessment of the murder weapon was the same, a short blunt billy club like instrument never left at the scene, The times of death were all similar, late night usually near midnight. The patterns were so similar it should have been an easy case, but the killer never make a mistake, at least not one that the great Jake Pageant could pick up. There were never any prints, any scraps of fabric, skin, nails, or hair. There never seemed to be struggle between the victim and his assailant. These derelicts were all so boozed up when they were murdered that there was no way they could have fought back.

There were also no claims or tips to the press, Mike explained to Gwen. Usually, serial killers want their work publicized. Usually, they crave the glamour of being talked up in the papers and on TV. They call TV stations. They leave notes around. They write long, deranged letters.

"But this guy just goes about his business and leaves us nothing." Mike concluded, his voice sounding so frustrated that it bordered on rage. "This guy's almost perfect, so far."

"So, you expected him to make a mistake?" Gwen asked.

"I do, but Jake doesn't expect it." Mike closed his eyes and formed his hands into angry fists. "Sometimes it's almost as if Jake's holding things from me. Like he knows more than he's telling me, but he's embarrassed to 'fess up that he's as stumped as he is."

"Why would he do that?"

Mike shrugged. "It's like the uniforms at the station say. Maybe Jake just doesn't want to solve this one. In a way it's busy work for a short timer. Maybe he's waiting for his retirement party. Maybe he just wants to solve it as a parting shot when he goes." He laughed softly under his breath.

Gwen couldn't laugh. Murder, even of homeless addicted alcoholics is no laughing matter. She realized how callous Mike had become since he started on this case. She realized how much he had changed.

An idea came to Gwen's head. "Subconsciously, maybe Jake knows who the killer is," she told Mike as she sipped the last of her coffee. "Maybe his mind is playing it safe, in a way. When I spoke to him, I remember how affected he was when his old partner died so close to retirement. I remember he was very upset about that and how he was adamant about that not happening to him. Maybe his subconscious is preventing him from solving this crime for his own safety.... or so it thinks."

"It???" Mike looked puzzled. "Who's it!?"

"His subconscious!" Gwen snapped back. She was proud of herself. Her quickness. Her sharp analytical mind.

"You're nuts. This is real life, not TV."

"Could be." she continued to smile. "Just could be."

* * * *

There was something eerie about the neighborhood at night. There was something in the cold, crisp stillness that caused goose bumps to climb up and down Gwen Smith's spine as she shivered against the cold. The temperature would plummet down to the teens this cold February night, but it was still hovering around freezing as she walked the darkened streets.

She had been poking around the neighborhood for the past few nights. She had talked to some of the homeless men who sought refuge on steam vents or in dark corners that sheltered them from the wind and the cold. She had talked to the shopkeepers on Kensington Avenue about the slow, agonizing decline of the neighborhood. She walked the sidewalks of the small side streets, each one looking like the last with their cracked cement and their little row homes.

It had been three weeks since the last murder and the police investigation was beginning to die down. They'd lost interest, or Jake had run out of ideas, and she knew that it was time for the killer to strike again. Whether Jake Pageant knew who the killer was or was just psychologically incapable of solving the string of murders, Gwen was determined to find some answers.

After all, she told herself each night as she braved the cold and her own fears, *isn't that what investigative journalism is all about?*

Gwen was scared to death but determined to follow through on her theory. She just had to take the chance, she knew, as she firmly gripped the can of mace in her gloved fist. Both hands were stuck in the pockets of her coat. She hadn't worn the fake fur, instead opting for her worn out wool coat that went out of date two years before, the one no one had seen.

She had parked her car in what looked like a relatively safe street a couple of blocks from K&A. The street looked clean and there were small lamp posts near each stoop to light the way, but there weren't many venturing out on this winter's night. Some people, yes, like the man walking his dog, both their breaths forming a cloud in the air as they quickly moved along. Like the construction worker returning home from work, his clothes caked with dirt and his face looking sour as he glanced her way.

Across the street on the corner, the news stand was being closed up and the old man who ran it was checking his padlocks and calling it quits for the night. She watched him from a distance as he made sure everything was secure and looked at the last of the commuters coming down from the El platform. One approached the old man and gestured frantically to him. Obviously, the commuter wanted a paper, but the old man....*what did Mike call him, Kozicki,* refused to open up. The commuter finally gave up, shook his head in disgust and turned away.

Kozicki watched him go, took a brown paper bag out of his coat pocket, unscrewed the lid of the bottle it held and took a swig. He then started up Allegheny Avenue at a slow gait.

For some reason, one she couldn't pin down, Gwen crossed over Kensington and followed him at a respectable distance. *Okay, Gwen,* she told herself, *don't be frightened.*

At the end of the block Kozicki stopped and turned to talk to a man lying on a steam vent. The bum got up from this seat and walked next to the old man. Gwen couldn't hear the words they said to each other, the noise of traffic and the wind was all that echoed in her ears, but she knew it was a heated argument from their gestures and the puffs of white smoke that formed around their heads.

She moved closer to the pair.

"I'm telling you," she overheard Kozicki say as she passed him. "Get off the street tonight, Fred. It's the coldest night of the winter, they say."

"Naw!" The other man scowled. "Just like every other night, I tell you. They just want to get me in so they can put me away."

"Ain't safe no more," Kozicki said as he again took the bottle from his pocket. He took some and handed it over to the other man.

"Thanks, Frank," she heard the other man say.

"Just get off the street, man," Frank replied.

Gwen turned the corner and stopped. Huddling against the side of the building she waited for Kozicki to pass her again.

She peaked around the corner.

His eyes met hers.

She jumped!

He smiled a toothless smile at her, nodded and passed her. "Sorry, Miss," he mumbled. "Didn't mean to scare you."

She turned and watched him move away, his short stubby form waddling as it went, the bottle in his pocket making a clanging sound as it hit his keys with each step.

The was close! Gwen caught her breath, swallowed her courage and continued after him at a respectable distance.

Two more blocks and two turns later, Gwen began to feel that she had followed the old man far enough. There was nothing moving on the street but the two of them, yet, although he must have known she was behind him, he never stopped and never looked back. His pace continued to be constant, even when he occasionally took the bottle out of this pocket and took another sip.

Gwen was growing nervous. She didn't know the neighborhood that well and knew a million good reasons to be afraid. Yet, her own curiosity had brought her down this path and her own stupidity kept her going. She didn't even know what she was looking for. Not really.

Up ahead, Kozicki had stopped and so Gwen stopped. *So, Mister, are you finally getting suspicious?* Her eyes remained focused on him as he turned.

Instead of turning her way he looked toward the alleyway as a dark figure quickly jumped out at the man. Gwen saw a club in the figure's hands. She saw Kozicki get hit.

Gwen clutched the mace tightly in one hand and fumbled for the police whistle in her pocket with her other hand. And she ran toward them.

Her footsteps were heard by the dark figure, who glanced up and vanished into the shadows from which he came.

"Stop!" she screamed as she got nearer. She blew the whistle as loud as she could.

As doors began to open in the row homes that lined the street, Gwen reached Kozicki. The old man was holding his head as blood oozed from between his fingers. His bottle of whiskey lay broken on the pavement, and he looked up at the girl with a dazed and surprised look.

But, he was alive.

* * * *

There was something about hospitals that always gave Mike Rossi the creeps. It was something in the air, he reasoned. The antiseptic cleanliness of the place? The white uniforms? He wasn't sure. Maybe it was the way the place smelled, like the inside of a band-aid that had been worn for two days.

Northeastern Hospital was no different than other hospitals. The old wing was like something out of an old movie. The new wing was like something out of a TV show, but both had the same smell, the same look and the same feel to Mike. He hated it and the way everyone looked at him when he went by. They knew he didn't like being there.

The emergency room had the usual stainless-steel furniture. It had the usual white shower curtain that was drawn around the cubicle that kept people outside from seeing in but didn't provide any real privacy. It had the usual assortment of white hospital things; gauze and bandages and tapes and papers and torn packages that all these things came in lying on the floor near the trash can. It had the usual sour faced nurse who was applying bandages to Frank Kozicki's head.

She looked even more sour when Mike flashed his badge and asked her to leave.

"Who hit you?" he quickly asked the old man.

"I don't know," Kozicki mumbled as he shifted himself around on the steel table.

"Do you know any reason this man would want to attack you?" Mike asked as he took out his little pad and pencil. He hoped he'd have something to write down.

"I don't know," Kozicki repeated.

"Look, Frank, it was late. It was dark. You had to be drinking. Do you think this guy could have mistaken you for one of the derelicts."

"You mean it could've been the guy who's been knocking off these bums." Kozicki suddenly had a sly smile across his toothless mouth.

"That's what I think," Mike said to Frank. Then, under his breath, he said to himself, "This could be his first mistake."

"Naw." Kozicki waved his news print stained hand at the cop. "Doesn't fit the picture. The killer's always hit the bums when they ain't looking. The killer's always made sure they were dead before he left. One, two blows ain't never been enough."

"But someone saw him, blew that whistle and busted it up."

"Yeah, that girl did......what's her name?"

"Gwen, Gwen Smith." Mike proudly answered, although he was mad as hell at her.

"Listen, kiddo," Kozicki rubbed his head. "I don't know who slugged me. I didn't see his face or nothing. He didn't leave nothing behind but the dent in my skull and cost me one, nearly full pint of Jack Daniels. I can't help you, kid, so leave me alone."

"Well, okay, Frank, but I may have some more questions later."

"Yeah, well, I ain't going nowhere," Kozicki said as he lifted himself off the table. "I'm dizzy as hell, Mikey. Get the nurse for me. I gotta take a leak."

After the nurse came Mike left the cubicle. Waiting outside the curtain was Gwen, who obviously had been listening to every word.

"He's lying," she immediately told Mike. "He knew who that guy was. He saw his face as clearly as you're seeing mine. He may have even spoke to him. I was too far away to hear."

"You can't say that for sure."

"Yes, Mike, I can," she insisted as they walked toward the front of the ER. "I saw them look each other in the eyes. It may have been dark, but they were just a couple of feet away from each other. I saw them look at each other, exchange nods and then the guy pulled out the club and hit him."

"How long was the club?" he asked her.

She spread her hands apart. "About this long. I don't know, Michael. It all happened so fast."

"If it happened so fast how come you're so sure that you saw them look at each other and talk?" he snapped at her.

"I just do."

They stopped at the door. "Gwen." Mike made his voice as serious as he could and stared deeply into her eyes. "You shouldn't have even been there. You know how dangerous this neighborhood can be. What were you thinking?"

"Michael, I....."

He cut her off. "Now I have to ask you to come to the station with me. I need a statement and I'm sure Jake will have a few questions when he gets in."

"Where is 'Joe Friday' anyway?"

"I don't know." Mike snapped as he took hold of her arm. "And shut up for a change, will you. You don't know how pissed I am at you."

* * * *

Gwen no longer cared what Detective Mike Rossi thought. In her heart she loved the man, the private Mike Rossi who laughed at her jokes and could guess her innermost thoughts, but the policeman that was his outer shell had told her to shut up and go home and that was something Gwen was not going to do.

She felt something was wrong with Frank Kozicki's story. He spoke too little about the man who attacked him. He knew too little about him. Gwen could have guessed his size and weight, and she was over fifty feet away at the time. Why couldn't Kozicki? She was certain he had seen his face and that he recognized it. The news stand owner said he couldn't tell who the attacker was. Why was Kozicki lying?

Gwen was going to find out.

They released Kozicki from the hospital the following day. Gwen, who had lied when she called the hospital to ask about his condition, missed him as he quietly left the hospital and now waited for him outside his small row house. She'd stay there as long as it took, or as long as her body would let her as the cold chill of winter blew through her old Chevy Nova.

She waited in the dark, bundled up in her coat and two layers of clothing, her hands curled around a cup of once hot coffee and hoped that her guess was right. Kozicki had to be out that night. He had to go out to find the man who assaulted him, maybe the man who committed the murders.

About ten-thirty her prayers were answered.

Frank Kozicki, wearing the same old wool coat, hat, and his knit gloves with the tips of the fingers cut out, came out of the row house and walked slowly up the street, the keys in his pockets sounding like jungle bells.

For twenty minutes she followed him in her car, and he never looked around. The engine of the car filled her ears as she eased it along. She stopped at the beginning of each block while Kozicki walked along and then waited until he'd turn the corner and crept up to that corner, poked her nose around and find out where he'd gone.

Why hasn't he grown suspicious? Why hasn't he turned around?

He moved along at his slow pace, never looking back, never stopping, his course absolutely determined.

He turned another corner.

Gwen softly stepped on the gas and crept up.

She looked around and he was nowhere to be found.

"Damn!" she said aloud to no one.

She moved along at five miles per hour and searched around three streets for the man, but he had given her the slip. Deliberately, she was sure.

Seeing a phone booth, she stopped the car, turned it off and took the keys. She called Mike but got his machine.

He had told me he was going to be home tonight, she thought. *He never misses Monday Night Football.*

Gwen left a message. "Michael. I know you'll be mad, but I'm down in Kensington. Kozicki's out and around. I followed him from this house and he's on his way. Michael, I know he's going to find the killer. I know he knows who he is. Michael, please come......."

She heard the second beep. The machine had stopped recording. She hung up the phone and listened as the last quarter dropped.

Gwen inhaled a gallon of cold winter's air and summoned up all her courage. Leaving her car, she continued on foot to find Frank Kozicki.

* * * *

It took only a few minutes, but Gwen's bones began to ache as she continued to search the streets. The temperature seemed to be dropping by the minute and the wind seemed to be picking up as quickly, at least to her. Slowly, she realized that a freezing rain had begun to fall, the cold icicles striking her face like a thousand needles.

I must be crazy, she told herself as she turned another corner, and convinced herself that it would be the last she would walk. Her car was nearby, waiting to shelter her from the cold. She yearned for the warmth, the hot air from its old heater breathing on her feet, the radio blasting in her ears. Now, it was only one block away.

Up ahead, a figure emerged from a darkened corner. Gwen didn't care, didn't even take notice of the man until she was nearly on top of him. He leered at her with a familiar sneer on his weather-beaten face. It was Detective Jake Pageant.

"What are you doing here?" she asked, her voice quivering, her teeth chattering with each syllable.

"I should ask you the same thing," he replied. His tone was cold and harsh. "But I won't."

Gwen felt her whole body shiver. "Well, I'm making a damned stupid fool out of myself and now I'm going home."

"No, Gwen, you're not," Jake said as he reached out and took hold of her arm.

Gwen felt his fist tighten and the jab of pain shot up her arm and quickly erased the cold. She felt another pair of arms on her, one arm around her waist and the other around her neck. She saw a hand, covered in a woolen glove with the fingers cut out.

"Too bad, little girl!" She heard Jake's voice as she struggled in vain against the arms surrounding her. Every movement caused a jolt of pain. Every inch that she pulled free seemed to tighten the grip of the hands capturing her. "You just got too close. You just couldn't let it alone, could you?"

Her attackers pulled her into an alley as she continued to struggle against their strength. Suddenly the arms seemed to let go of her, but she felt herself flung against the brick wall of the alley. She felt the rough damp brick surface against her skin as it scraped her face. Her breath seemed to be sucked out of her lungs.

Dizzy, her eyes unable to focus, she felt only her own heartbeat. Gwen collapsed to the base of the brick wall. As she struggled against the pain, she turned herself around and focused on her attackers.

A single white light illuminated the alley way. In it, standing above her, their fists clenched, their heavy breathing emitting puffs of white smoke just as if they were dragons, were Jake Pageant and Frank Kozicki.

"Why'd you have to keep nosing around?" Jake asked. "Why couldn't you just stay out of it?"

"What???" Gwen mumbled, unable to grasp the meaning of his questions.

"Come on, Jake." Kozicki said, his voice sounding nervous. "Let's get this over with."

"We had a good plan." Pageant continued. "We had it all made."

Finally, Gwen seemed to understand what the man was saying. "You killed them. Both of you."

"Give the girl a prize," Pageant sneered. "Frank and I had it all planned. No danger. No chance winding up like my old partner, dead before he could enjoy his retirement. I wasn't going to take any chances, Missy. I was going to make it. I only had a short time left."

"You're wasting time." Kozicki whined.

"We've got lots of time, Frank," Pageant snapped. "Who's going to help her, anyway?"

Gwen thought about her phone call to Michael. *Where was he? Would be come in time? Stall! Stall, Gwen, it could mean your life.*

"You were a good cop, Jake, why'd you do it?" she asked.

"The first bum, he was a mistake." Pageant answered, his voice arrogant and seemingly proud of what he was telling her. "Just got too angry. Then Frank and me, we planned to retire to the cabin that Marty and I had built. I'd lose that if they knew I killed a man, even if he was a wino, even if he was dirtying up the neighborhood. So, the first one, we covered up and the rest just kept it going. I only had a short time left; you know. It got easier as time went by."

"It was only a few useless old bums," Kozicki added. "It cleaned up the neighborhood."

"Yeah," Jack sneered. "A public service."

"And we'd have gotten away with it, too, if you hadn't started snooping around." Kozicki pointed at Gwen. "No one would have suspected. Only an outsider like you."

"Why'd you follow Frank that night, Gwen?" Pageant asked. "Why'd you do a stupid thing like that?"

"On a whim," Gwen answered.

"You got too close," Kozicki said.

"And now we have to kill you," Pageant added.

They took a step toward her, and Gwen frantically pulled herself back, but the wall of the alley blocked any retreat and there was nowhere to go. She clung to the brick face and waited for them, her eyes closed, and her teeth clenched.

"Gwen!" a voice shouted off in the distance. It was Mike's voice.

"Jeez!" Kozicki jumped.

"It's Rossi," Jake sneered. "But he's too late."

Gwen could feel their breath as they grew closer.

"Gwen!" She heard Mike's voice again.

"Michael!" she screamed. A hand cupped itself over her mouth, shutting off the screams that were about to come out.

She bit hard on the gloved hand, and it released itself from her mouth.

"Michael!" she screamed again.

"Damned!" a voice yelled. "She bit me!"

She struggled past the men, their arms reaching for her as she bolted. Just before she reached the mouth of the alleyway, she felt them get a hold around her waist.

"Mi....!" she began, but her screams were cut short as a lightning bolt of pain shot from her back and shuddered throughout her body.

She looked down at her chest and saw the faintest sliver of a knife coming through. It was lined with a red ribbon of blood. Her blood! It was the last thing she remembered.

* * * *

She awoke to the sounds of his voice. It began like a soft murmur in the back of her mind, summoning her from darkness, from hopelessness.

"Gwen," his voice whispered. "Gwen, can you hear me?"

Her mind slowly began to tell itself that it was time to wake up. Her eyes opened slowly and focused on the face in front of her.

"Gwen, can you hear me?" he quietly repeated.

"Yes, Michael," she felt herself smile as she spoke the words. "I can."

You were right, Gwen," she heard him say. "Kozicki was lying. He did know who committed the murders."

"Michael, I'm sorry," she whimpered. Gwen felt the tears roll down her cheeks.

"You'll be okay, Gwen," Michael comforted her, his hands softly touching her hair. "He knifed you, but it luckily missed your heart. Don't worry, darling, you're in the hospital and safe. We got him. He's dead."

"We?" Gwen whimpered, feeling weak and unable to fully compose her thoughts.

"You just rest and be still, Gwen," Michael reassured her, his face smiling down at her. "I've got to get the doctor."

His face left her view and she weakly tried to lift her head to follow him out of the room.

"Jake will be here if you need anything."

Another face appeared over her bed. He had the same familiar, cold, leering smile.

"Don't worry, Missy. I'll take care of you," Jake Pageant said.

Gwen tried to scream as he placed the pillow over her face, but it was hopeless.